THE PERFECT HUSBAND

Five years ago, Melanie's drunken husband died in a car crash, nearly taking her baby son with him. Since then, she's not entrusted her heart to anyone, but aware that her son needs adult male company, she asks her boss, Jack, to fill that role. However, Jack longs to make the three of them a proper family. On a romantic trip to the Amalfi Coast in Italy, he hopes that Melanie, forgetting her fears, will learn to trust him . . .

HELEN SCOTT TAYLOR

THE PERFECT HUSBAND

Complete and Unabridged

LINFORD
Leicester

First published in Great Britain in 2011

First Linford Edition
published 2013

British Library CIP Data

Taylor, Helen Scott.
   The perfect husband.- -
(Linford romance library)
1. Love stories.
2. Large type books.
I. Title II. Series
823.9'2–dc23

ISBN 978–1–4448–1435–4

Published by
F. A. Thorpe (Publishing)
Anstey, Leicestershire

Set by Words & Graphics Ltd.
Anstey, Leicestershire
Printed and bound in Great Britain by
T. J. International Ltd., Padstow, Cornwall

This book is printed on acid-free paper

1

'Ooh la la, Mr Scrumptious is back — and he's tanned. Wonder if he's bronzed all over?' the hotel receptionist warbled in a suggestive voice and waggled her eyebrows.

Standing in the foyer of the Greyfriar House Hotel where she was manager, Melanie Marshall peered towards the window looking out over the car park.

Sure enough, her boss, Jack Summers, was unloading his bags from the boot of his Mercedes. The sun glinted off his neat golden hair as he turned away from the main hotel and pulled his case towards The Gatehouse where he lived.

'Where's the other half of the golden twins, I wonder?' the receptionist asked, using the nickname the staff had given to Jack and his blonde fiancée, Stephanie.

Walking closer to the window, Melanie checked outside. 'Stephanie's definitely not with him.'

Jack and Stephanie were due to be married in Barbados any day now. Melanie had been so busy during the last few days she'd lost track of the wedding date. She went to the reception desk and checked the calendar; today was Tuesday.

'Isn't Jack's wedding supposed to be on the twenty-third of May . . . tomorrow?'

The receptionist glanced over Melanie's shoulder. 'You're right.' They shared a puzzled look. 'If Jack's supposed to be in Barbados marrying Stephanie, what on earth is he doing back in England alone?'

Melanie gave a non-committal shrug, unwilling to speculate further on Jack's personal life with other members of staff.

She gnawed her lip as she retreated to the manager's office, took her seat and started sorting through the heap of documents requiring her attention: two complaints from guests who'd stayed the weekend the water was cut off because of a leak, a letter of recommendation and three wedding bookings.

Unable to concentrate, she dropped the papers back on her desk, wandered to the window and stared at Jack's car.

What was going on? Why had he returned early? She hated the kind of uncertainty that might affect her job as well as her living arrangements.

Jack had taken her on to manage Greyfriar House in his stead because he expected to have less time for work once he married. If he hadn't tied the knot, did that mean she'd be out of a job? She'd have trouble finding another position in this small Devon town that paid as well and came with accommodation. Perhaps she was worrying about nothing and Jack and Stephanie had simply postponed their wedding.

The Queen Anne clock on the mantelpiece chimed the hour. She quickly found her handbag and changed out of her smart, heeled shoes into flats to walk down the hill to meet her six-year-old son, Ryan, when he came out of school.

On her way out past the reception desk, she updated the duty manager who'd arrived to take responsibility for the hotel when she finished her shift at three. That done, she walked briskly down the drive.

As she passed Jack's gatehouse, from the corner of her eye she caught a flash of movement in an upstairs window and tension crawled up her spine. Why had Jack changed his plans? What would it mean for her and Ryan?

She loved her job and the comfortable flat she and Ryan occupied over the old stables. It felt more like home than any of the numerous places they had stayed during the past five years. She pulled in a deep calming breath and told herself not to worry until she had something to worry about.

As she passed between the imposing stone pillars marking the hotel entrance, and hurried along the road towards the school, she told herself that whatever happened she would do her best for Ryan. She owed that to her darling little boy — he was the only thing that mattered in her life now.

★ ★ ★

Jack stood back in the shadows of his bedroom and watched Melanie's slender form stride purposefully past his cottage and through the gate, her luxuriant chestnut hair flying behind her. She wasn't blatantly glamorous like Stephanie, but she had an aura of energy and enthusiasm that people responded to. Hotel guests liked her and his staff worked hard for her. When he'd employed her to step into his shoes, he'd had high expectations and she'd proved to be worth her weight in gold. Now, through his own stupidity, he might lose her services.

A jolt of feeling passed through him, and he put it down to worry over the possibility of losing his best employee.

With a sigh, he unzipped his case, removed his white tuxedo and hung it on the wardrobe door. He stood back and stared at it, his mind a dazed fog from jet lag and confusion over his feelings for Stephanie.

His mother had pushed and pushed until he agreed to marry Stephanie. He'd thought he'd recovered from his bad memories of his first love, Marianne, and was ready to marry — until he arrived in Barbados to be faced with the wedding preparations.

Stephanie hadn't wanted to listen when he voiced his doubts, so he'd panicked and told her he was in love with another woman. When she grilled him for a name, he had blurted out Melanie Marshall. He had no idea why his hotel manager's name had popped into his head at that moment, but it had done the trick and Stephanie had released him.

But he'd not only dug himself out of one hole and into another, but now he had to admit his faux pas to Melanie and find a way to apologise.

* * *

The following morning, Melanie was finishing up a tour with a couple thinking of booking the hotel for their wedding reception, when Jack wandered in. Out of the corner of her eye, she watched him exchange a few words with the girl on reception, then disappear into the manager's office and close the door. So much for that becoming her office when he married!

She shook hands with the young couple and saw them to the door then, sighing, she walked back to the office.

Despite telling herself she'd overcome much worse problems, she'd spent a restless night tossing and turning, worrying about the future of her job and the implications for her son if she couldn't find another position near his school.

She raised her hand to knock, then changed her mind. What the heck; this was supposed to be her office. She pushed the door open to find Jack staring out the window, hands in his trouser pockets.

He glanced over his shoulder, flashing a quick smile of white teeth against tanned skin, and sparkling blue eyes. She felt an echo of the strange jolt of awareness she had experienced the first time she met him. With a sharp breath, she straightened her shoulders.

Many of the female members of staff flirted with Jack, but Melanie liked to think she was immune to his good looks and charm. After all, he was her boss; that alone made him out-of-bounds in her book. Plus he'd been engaged to be married.

'Come in, Melanie,' he said, turning to face her.

'I'm already in.' She raised her eyebrows and halted by the side of the desk.

'So you are.' He crossed his arms and leaned back against the windowsill. 'I expect you'd like to know what's going on.'

8

'I have been wondering.' She hoped he was about to explain there'd been a minor delay in the wedding plans and he would be married in a couple of weeks.

He briefly looked away and flattened his lips. Before he even said a word, she sensed the problems with his marriage plans amounted to more than a minor delay.

'I'll be coming back here to work full-time,' he said, his voice determined.

Her worst fears realised, Melanie stepped across to one of the velvet guest chairs and dropped onto the seat. How could she persuade him to keep her on? Maybe if she accepted a lesser position? As long as she kept the manager's flat, she'd survive on less pay. Possibilities spun through her mind.

'I want you to stay on.' He walked closer and propped a hip against the edge of the desk. 'I'd been thinking about trying to secure more corporate events before this wedding malarkey took over my life. I want you to continue managing the wedding reception side of the business while I explore the corporate angle. I've got the contacts . . . ' He winced. 'Or at least I did have before I jilted the town's favourite solicitor. Let's just hope Stephanie isn't the sort to take revenge by sabotaging my business reputation.'

Melanie leaned back on a sigh and the tension in her shoulders eased. 'That's a relief. I thought you wouldn't want me any more.'

Jack swallowed audibly then looked down at his feet and cleared his throat. 'I don't want you to suffer because I temporarily seem to have lost the plot. Your job will remain unchanged, except we'll be sharing this office. I'm sure we can manage to work around each other.' He glanced up at her from beneath his lashes.

'I'm sure we can,' she said briskly, ignoring the way his eyes appeared even bluer than usual against his tanned skin.

Jack straightened his tie and she got the distinct impression he was feeling

10

uncomfortable. That wasn't surprising considering the situation. It couldn't be easy discussing one's personal life with a member of staff.

Whatever had caused Jack to change his mind about getting married was none of her business, and she had no intention of prying. If he wanted to confide in her, he could, but that was unlikely. They hardly knew each other. Their relationship was strictly professional. And would continue to be.

Melanie breathed a sigh of relief and stood, suddenly full of enthusiasm for the rest of the day's work. The happy life she and Ryan were establishing in this new town would continue. Day-by-day, week-by-week they would put the past behind them.

Then she noticed the time on the clock over the fireplace.

'I'm afraid I have to go; I have a one o'clock appointment and I'd like to grab a sandwich first if that's all right with you?'

Jack's gaze skimmed over her thoughtfully. 'There's something we need to discuss, Melanie, but I suppose it can wait until later.'

She didn't like his ominous tone of voice, but her position as manager was safe and anything else paled into insignificance beside that worry.

He waved her away, and she strode towards the door. Hard work kept her mind off the past and this job was nothing if not busy. That was why she enjoyed it so much.

*   *   *

The following day, Melanie was sitting at one of the tables in the dining room with a sales rep, examining new wedding table-decorations, when a waitress brought her a business card.

Melanie turned the square of vellum into the light and read the elegant script, *Ms Stephanie Curtis, Solicitor.* She held it out to the waitress with a smile. 'I think this is meant for Jack. He's lunching with the Rotary Club chairman. Why don't you suggest she rings him later?'

The waitress shook her head, blonde curls bouncing. 'No, the lady specifically asked for you.'

Melanie frowned. 'Are you sure?'

When the young woman nodded, Melanie apologised to the sales rep and told him she would consider his products and be in touch soon.

With a hint of trepidation, Melanie walked out to the reception area — she couldn't imagine what Stephanie Curtis could possibly want with her. She'd only met the woman a few times. Usually she saw her from a distance as she came and went from Jack's house. The last thing she wanted was to get involved in their relationship problems.

Stephanie Curtis rose elegantly from a floral settee by the huge granite fireplace in the entrance hall and offered her hand politely as Melanie approached.

'May we talk?'

Melanie could hardly say no, so she led her visitor into the manager's office

13

and closed the door. 'Please take a seat.'

Not sure if this visit should be classed as business or personal, Melanie opted to take the second guest chair rather than sit on the other side of the desk. As soon as she sat and noticed Stephanie's chilly expression, she wished she'd put the barrier of the desk between them.

'How can I help you, Ms Curtis?' she asked.

Stephanie glanced around the room, her glossy, pink lips taut, her eyes narrowed.

'Did you do it in here?' she asked suddenly.

She gave Melanie a derisive glance and laughed bitterly. 'No, you don't look the sort to be so risqué. I bet you're an 'in bed with the lights out' type of gal, aren't you? What on earth does Jack see in you?'

For several moments Melanie couldn't think, the quiet tick of the clock marking off the seconds as she stared at Stephanie, mouth open, her brain frozen in shock.

'I don't know — '

'Please spare me the pointless denials,' Stephanie interrupted as she jumped up and stalked around the room, examining the furnishings as if she were picturing Melanie and Jack together in various places.

'You really have got this wrong.' Melanie stood and followed Stephanie. 'There's nothing between Jack and me. Nothing . . . heavens . . . ' Melanie put her hand to her throat and flushed at the thought of Jack getting close to her, touching her. 'Whoever told you this is just out to cause trouble, I'm sure. I promise there's no truth in it. How can you even imagine he'd be interested in someone like me?'

She reined back the denials crowding her mind. She was babbling and needed to calm down.

Stephanie stared at her through narrowed eyes, her expression dangerous. 'Don't lie to me. Jack himself told me he's in love with you.'

'Jack? In love with me?' Melanie stumbled back and caught hold of the edge of the desk. 'Why would Jack say . . . ?'

Stephanie pointed a finger at her. 'Don't think you're getting away with this. Everyone thinks you're such a nice person. And isn't Jack lucky to have found someone he can trust to take care of his precious hotel! It looks like Jack got lucky in more ways than one, doesn't it? Well I'm going to make sure everyone knows exactly what sort of unscrupulous woman you really are.'

'But I'm not . . . ' Melanie began, but one look at Stephanie's face told her she was wasting her breath.

Stephanie strode towards the door. 'Tell Jack I said hi when you see him.' Then she slammed the door behind her.

Melanie stared blankly at the fireplace for a long time, trying to absorb what had just happened. The hollow, breathless shock inside her gradually filled with spiky anger.

Nothing had happened between her and Jack, which meant that for some reason he'd lied and used her as an excuse to break off his engagement with Stephanie. When he got back from his lunch appointment, he had some explaining to do.

Melanie tried to work, but every time she started to read, her mind wandered back to her conversation — or should that be confrontation — with Stephanie.

Jack himself told me he's in love with you.

Ridiculous as Stephanie's words sounded, she couldn't forget them. There was no way Jack had feelings for her. Absolutely no way. She'd have noticed some clue in his behaviour, surely? Even if he did love her, what difference did that make? She was certainly not in the market for a husband, or even a boyfriend. And even if she were, she knew better than to date her boss.

Even if he did look like a god.

The thought crossed her mind completely unbidden as if even her own mind was trying to betray her, and a little frisson of something she'd rather ignore ran up and down her spine.

She gave herself a shake, sat up straight, and tried to concentrate on the letter she was composing, but every time she heard a car, her gaze skipped across to the window to check if it was Jack.

When she finally spied the silver Mercedes pull up in a parking space outside, she shot out of her seat and headed for the door, a ball of nervous tension wound tight in her belly.

Thank goodness he'd come back before she had to collect Ryan from school. If she'd had to sleep on this without confronting him first, she'd have had a terrible night.

She hurried out the front door and met him as he headed towards the hotel. 'May I have a word?' she said briskly.

He turned his bone-melting smile on her. 'Certainly.' He indicated she should precede him through the hotel door, but she held her ground.

'I'd rather talk somewhere a little

more private if you don't mind.' Melanie had a nasty feeling this conversation might involve raised voices, and she didn't want the staff knowing her business. At least, not yet, anyway. Although if Stephanie got her way, it sounded as though she intended to spread the news of Melanie's supposed relationship with Jack around the whole town, so the staff would hear eventually.

For a moment he hesitated, surprise and a touch of caution on his face. Then he changed course towards his house. 'Let's go to the Gatehouse. We shouldn't be disturbed there.'

He opened his front door then stood aside to let her pass. The thought suddenly hit her that this was the first time she'd been inside his house. If anyone saw them, this would apparently confirm Stephanie's allegations.

Melanie wrung her hands together as she paced across the small living room to the window and looked out over the neatly manicured lawn at the back of the property.

She heard Jack moving around behind her and closed her eyes. How on earth did you accuse a man of claiming to love you? Especially when it was patently obvious that he didn't. Maybe it would be easiest to give him the chance to come clean with her first.

'Would you like a cup of tea?' he asked. She realised he was very close behind her and his nearness hummed over her skin like an electric charge in the air.

'No.' She shook her head and bit her lip.

'Unfortunately, I think I might know what this is about.'

The wariness in his voice sent goose bumps racing down her arms. She'd hoped to discover Stephanie's accusation was a misunderstanding, but Jack's voice clearly held an unmistakable hint of guilt.

'Ms Curtis came to see me today,' she began carefully.

He cursed softly, a word she'd never heard him use before. 'Sorry,' he added quickly. 'What did she say?'

'Perhaps you could tell me what do you think she said?'

'I'd prefer not to play guessing games.'

Sudden anger snapped through her at the exasperation in his voice. She jerked around and met his intense blue gaze with a level and accusing glare of her own. 'I'm not the one playing games. You've got some explaining to do.'

He raked his hands back through his hair with a sigh. 'I really am sorry if Stephanie's been unpleasant to you. I had no intention of involving you in our break-up. Quite frankly, I'm at a loss myself to know why I did. I can only apologise.'

Melanie shook her head as if in a daze, hearing his words but hardly able to believe them.

Jack gave her a slightly harassed look. 'It was a moment of madness, I assure you. Stephanie is very determined to get what she wants. Saying I'd fallen in love with another woman was the only way to extract myself from the relationship.'

'But why me?' Melanie rubbed her temples, comprehending the dilemma in which he'd found himself, yet still at a loss to understand why he'd picked on her.

Jack paced away and pinched the bridge of his nose. 'I've absolutely no idea. It's not as if I've thought of you in that way. I suppose you were on my mind because we work together.'

That confirmed what she'd thought. They had a strictly professional relationship. Irrationally, his explanation still bruised some sensitive female part of her that had hoped he at least found her slightly attractive.

'I assume she was angry?' he said.

'That barely begins to describe it. Spitting tacks, more like. She made certain allegations about my character and accused us of . . . of inappropriate behaviour.'

He'd been staring at the floor, but his

gaze shot up at her words. 'What exactly did she say?'

Heat burned up Melanie's neck into her face. She opened her mouth to speak and then closed it again.

'I'm sorry. Of course you don't have to elaborate.'

Mortified when tears flooded her eyes, she turned her back on him and dashed the tears away with the side of her hand.

'You must go and set this straight with Ms Curtis before she tells everyone,' she pleaded. 'If people in this town spread nasty gossip about me, it's bound to reach Ryan.'

At the thought of her six-year-old son's brave little face, tears clogged her throat again and burned the back of her nose. He'd already suffered enough to last a lifetime.

Jack put his hands on her shoulders and squeezed. She stepped away from him. If he put his arms around her to comfort her, she'd lose her battle to control her tears and Jack Summers was not a suitable shoulder to cry on.

She hadn't accepted the comfort of a man's arms since her husband had died five years ago. She couldn't afford to lean on a man again and be so disappointed.

With a huge effort, Melanie regained her composure. She needed to take a mental step back and be careful. She didn't want to lose her job over this situation.

After she blew her nose, she turned to face Jack and looked him in the eye. 'What we need now is damage control.'

If she pretended the situation was a work problem, it would make her feel better. The secret was to distance herself from the issue so that she could be objective.

'Damage control . . . ' he repeated with a frown. 'In this day and age, I think you're probably worrying unnecessarily. The towns people may gossip about us for a week or so but it will soon blow over and be forgotten about.'

Jack might dismiss gossip, but Melanie had first-hand experience of how damaging people's opinions could be, even if they were wrong. 'I won't take the chance that any bad feeling affects Ryan,' she said.

He rubbed his lips thoughtfully and scrutinised her for so long she feared he would see behind the façade she presented to the world and guess she was hiding something. She needed to divert his attention.

'We must meet with Stephanie and tell her the truth of the matter,' Melanie suggested.

'Ah.' Jack rubbed the back of his neck. 'I don't fancy our chances there. Once she's made up her mind about — '

'We'll go together. You can explain what happened, and I'll back you up.' Melanie could visualise the meeting.

They would book an appointment with Stephanie in her office to make it businesslike. Jack would calmly explain he'd felt cornered and said the first name that came to mind as an excuse to break off their relationship.

His explanation seemed plausible if a little stupid, but then she'd known men do far worse things under pressure. Hopefully Stephanie would be able to look at the situation in the same way and life could return to normal.

2

The following day, Jack led Melanie out of the hotel towards his car for their eleven o'clock appointment with Stephanie. Melanie crossed her fingers hoping Stephanie hadn't spread too much unsavoury gossip about them since she returned home.

Melanie slid into the passenger's seat of Jack's car and smoothed down the skirt of her sensible navy suit. She was aiming for a demure look. There was no point in antagonising Stephanie any more than necessary.

Out of the corner of her eye, Melanie caught sight of the hotel handyman staring after them as they drove away. Although Jack had taken Melanie out in the hotel's van to visit suppliers, she'd never ridden in his car before. His car was for personal use. Now the handyman had seen them leave together, it would be all over the hotel by the end of the day; validation for the gossip Stephanie had threatened to spread.

When they arrived at Stephanie's office, they were shown to a small waiting area with black and tan leather chairs. Jack fetched them both a cup of coffee from the machine, then sat with his chin in his hand staring out the window.

After a while, Melanie checked her watch for the third time and re-crossed her legs in the opposite direction. She wanted to get this wretched meeting over with and sort out the misunder- standing. 'I suspect there's a bit of one-upmanship going on here,' she said. 'She's kept us waiting nearly half an hour now.'

Jack turned her way, his gaze alighting on her legs. He stared for a second, then blinked as if coming out of a trance and sucked in a breath. 'Steph's probably running late. She always used to complain about her workload.'

At last, the receptionist showed them through. Stephanie was seated behind a contemporary expanse of glass and steel that passed for a desk. She didn't bother to stand to greet them. Stunning in a lavender suit and dove grey blouse, she rolled back her ergonomic chair and sensuously crossed her legs, exposing a length of slender thigh. She obviously wanted to show Jack what he was missing.

Melanie felt invisible in her functional navy suit and suddenly wished she hadn't been so practical.

'Take a seat.' Stephanie indicated the steel and leather guest chairs. Melanie perched stiffly on the edge of one, while Jack remained standing, hands clasped behind his back.

'To what do I owe this pleasure?' Stephanie asked in a tone that left no doubt their visit was anything but a pleasure.

'I want to clarify something.' Jack looked down at his feet, looking guilty before he even opened his mouth. Why was this so difficult for him? He was only setting the record straight.

'I'm afraid I wasn't entirely honest with you in Barbados, Stephanie,' he continued.

Stephanie shifted position and her glossy pink lips quirked. 'Jack Summers not telling the truth? Now there's a first.'

'I implicated Melanie in something she's not involved with.'

Melanie closed her eyes and took a steadying breath. *Just say it, Jack*, she urged him mentally.

'I'm not in love with Melanie. I used her name because I needed a good reason to back out of the wedding. I couldn't just say I'd got cold feet.'

'Why not?' Stephanie fired back.

The challenge seemed to galvanise Jack. He rested his hands on the desk and leant forwards. 'Because you'd have argued incessantly until you changed my mind, Steph.'

For long seconds, the two of them stared each other down and Melanie dared not move as tension thrummed in the air.

Eventually, Stephanie drew a delicate breath and looked away. 'You're right.'

'You might even have persuaded me to go ahead with the wedding and we'd have lived to regret it.'

She smiled slowly. 'Yes. I can be very persuasive, can't I?' From her sensual smile, Stephanie's thoughts had clearly wandered onto personal memories of her time with Jack. Focusing back on the room, Stephanie glanced from Jack to Melanie. 'So that's it? That's all you've come to say?'

Jack nodded and stepped back. The tension in Melanie's shoulders eased.

Stephanie held up a manicured, pink-nailed finger. 'One question puzzles me.' She pointed at Melanie. 'Why her? If you were using your imagination to make up a lover, surely you could have come up with someone a little more exciting.'

The insult rankled, especially as Stephanie had just voiced Melanie's own opinion. Both women looked at Jack and he shrugged, bewildered. 'No idea. Her name just came to mind.'

Stephanie drummed her nails on her blotter and the expression on her face sent a tingle of warning up Melanie's spine. 'If there's nothing between you two, why are you here as a couple? Look at you. Crazy as it sounds, there's chemistry between you.'

Chemistry! Melanie gulped and tried to come up with a retort, but words deserted her. Stephanie stood and pointed at the door. 'You made your bed, metaphorically and physically, Jack Summers. I suggest you lie in it and stop whining.'

'But there's nothing between us.' Melanie tried a last ditch plea as Stephanie strode to the door and held it open.

As Melanie stood, Jack put his hand on her back and eased her towards the door. He bent and whispered in her ear, 'I suggest you give it up.'

'But you've got to believe us.'

Melanie could hardly find enough air to force out the words.

Stephanie cast an accusing glance at Jack's hand on Melanie's back. 'I see through lies. I'm a solicitor, you see — it goes with the territory.'

A rush of despair washed through Melanie as Jack pushed her out onto the pavement.

'That was a spectacular failure,' he said, grimacing.

'How did it go so wrong?' Melanie sagged against the wall, her hand to her heart.

'There is chemistry between us, though. Did you know that?' He waggled his eyebrows in a way that was so out of character it looked ridiculous.

Because she could either laugh or cry and bursting into tears wasn't an option, Melanie gave a small breathless laugh. Then Jack's eyes crinkled at the corners and he chuckled. The knot of tension inside her loosened and she found herself laughing properly.

He angled his head and gave her a crooked smile. 'As we're obviously a lost cause and the whole town will soon know it, can I buy you lunch?'

'Why not?' Feeling light-headed, Melanie concentrated on breathing slowly as Jack led her towards the Lamb and Lion pub across the road.

'Let's refrain from discussing our relationship problems over lunch.' Jack grinned as he held the pub door open and placed his hand lightly on her back. Acutely aware of the pressure of his palm, she glanced around to check if anyone was watching them. As they walked through the bar and found a seat in a snug corner, no one gave them a second look.

The Stephanie problem faded from Melanie's mind as they talked. Jack related the trials and tribulations of converting the old Edwardian manor house into his hotel. She wished she could have been there to share the excitement. For an hour, the world stood still. Melanie couldn't remember the last time she had felt quite so carefree and relaxed.

* * *

It was only later in the evening that the potential consequences of their failure to convince Stephanie not to spread nasty gossip hit home.

Melanie fetched her old journal from her bedside table and cradled the shiny grey binding in her hand, letting it fall open at a random page. She scanned the words, reliving the pain and humiliation from five years ago when she and Ryan had been shunned by her mother and father and the people she had once called friends. Closing the book with a snap, she clutched it tightly and went to the door of Ryan's bedroom.

He looked so small in the big bed. The scars on his neck from the accident were faded but still visible above the collar of his pyjamas; the scars on his soul invisible to everyone but her.

She would never be able to forgive Jack if Stephanie said anything nasty that got back to Ryan and made her little boy unhappy again.

* * *

Two days later, Melanie was down on her knees in the hotel dining room with an old stain-removing recipe of her grandmother's in a plastic bowl, dabbing at a nasty mark on the carpet. Her first warning she had a visitor was a booming female voice: the sort of voice that belonged to a woman who wanted everyone in the room to stop and listen to her.

The receptionist appeared at the dining-room door and gave a strained smile. 'Visitor for you, Melanie.'

Melanie stood and wiped her hands on a paper towel. 'I've no one booked in.'

A statuesque woman clad in primrose silk the same shade as her hair appeared in the doorway behind the receptionist.

'I don't need an appointment.' She strode past the receptionist and held out a bejewelled hand. 'Am I addressing Melanie Marshall?' She shook hands with a surprisingly tight grip. 'I'm Imelda Summers. We need to talk, Mrs Marshall.'

A flash of shock tightened Melanie's stomach. 'Oh — you're Jack's mother?'

The woman cocked an eyebrow and appraised her. 'You have it in one. Now the office is the best place to talk, I think. This way.' She marched out of the dining room towards the office as though she owned the place.

Melanie patted her hair and glanced down at her dress, smoothing out the creases. A visit from Jack's mother couldn't be good, especially while Jack was twenty miles away meeting potential clients.

When they reached the office, Melanie halted in the open doorway and watched Mrs Summers prowl around, scanning the furniture in much the same way Stephanie had. Melanie sincerely hoped Mrs Summers's thoughts weren't following the same direction as Stephanie's had.

'Jack's not here, I'm afraid,' she said.

'Perfect. We'll have a girls' chat. Sit down.' She beckoned Melanie over to one of the guest chairs and, once she'd ordered coffee and closed the door, joined her.

'I expect you know why I'm here?'

'I have an idea, but you might have been misled.'

'Misled about what? About Jack walking out on his fiancée two days before his wedding because he claimed to be in love with you? Are you telling me that didn't happen?'

'Well yes, it happened. But Jack made a mistake.'

'You're absolutely right he made a mistake. Three years wasted.' She sighed and rose to walk to the window. 'I had high hopes for Stephanie and Jack, you know. I thought there were finally going to be grandchildren in my future. Then Jack fell at the final fence.

He's just like his father. No staying power. Now I'll have to start again with you.'

'Me?' Melanie's indignant response was partially drowned out by the sound of a knock on the door, which was probably a good thing.

Mrs Summers swept elegantly across to the door and carried the coffee tray back to the table herself. 'Don't want any prying ears,' she whispered conspiratorially as she poured two cups and added cream.

She handed a cup to Melanie, pursed her lips and stared thoughtfully into the distance. 'We need a plan of action.'

'To stop the gossip, you mean?'

'Gossip?' The woman flapped a hand. 'Forget the gossip, dear. Nobody will give a fig once you're family.'

'Family?'

'Am I not making myself clear? You seem a decent enough girl, and at this stage in the game, I'll take whatever I can get. We need to persuade Jack to marry you.'

'Oh, no!' Melanie shot out of her seat like a jack-in-a-box. Coffee spilled down the side of her dress, but she hardly cared. 'I'm not marrying anyone.'

'Why ever not? You're not still married, are you?'

'No — no, I'm not,' Melanie stammered. 'I'm a widow.'

'Well, good — although I'm sorry for your loss, of course. I assume it happened a few years ago?'

Melanie stared at the other woman nonplussed. She'd read about people spluttering with indignation, but she'd never known quite what it meant until this moment when she couldn't untie her tongue to form a coherent sentence.

Unable to think of anything else to do, she walked to the door and put her hand on the handle. 'I'd like you to leave. You need to discuss this with Jack, not me.'

Mrs Summers drew herself up in her chair and her friendly demeanour hardened. 'I hope you're not going to

40

fight me on this. If you love Jack, for Heaven's sake, why don't you want to marry him?'

Melanie ground her teeth and then forced herself to relax. 'I don't love Jack,' she said steadily.

'You don't love him, yet you've been sleeping with him? Perhaps Stephanie was right about you.'

'I'm not — ' Melanie paused and lowered her voice before the whole staff heard her denial. 'I'm not sleeping with Jack.'

Mrs Summers frowned as if Melanie had addressed her in a foreign language. Then her expression cleared and she smiled. 'Well, that's lovely. Young people have such loose morals these days. It's refreshing to discover some still willing to wait for marriage before they become intimate.'

Melanie sagged against the door and jammed a hand through her hair. Whatever she said, Jack's mother only heard what she wanted to hear.

'Jack doesn't like to tell people this,

but I own twenty-five percent of his hotel.' Mrs Summers looked around with pride. 'It certainly turned out to be a wise investment. Jack's done wonders with the place.' Mrs Summers stood and straightened her pearls. 'You'll come to our family dinner on Sunday, naturally. They're all dying to meet you.'

'I can't.'

'Of course you can. Jack will bring you so you don't need directions.' Mrs Summers glided elegantly towards the door and put a restraining hand on Melanie's arm as she pulled the door open. 'As a shareholder, I have some say in staffing decisions, dear. Don't let me down. I'd hate to see you lose your job when you've been such an asset to the business.'

Then she was through the door and gone with a flourish of yellow silk and a waft of some expensive scent.

Melanie stared after her, feeling as though she'd been run over by a designer steamroller. What had just happened? Had Jack's mother really blackmailed her into attending a Summers' family dinner by threatening her job?

Melanie closed her eyes and rested her head against the door. As far as possible, she'd kept her private life separate from work. She didn't want Ryan to get attached to anyone in case the past caught up with them and they had to move on. Now she'd have to introduce him to Jack and all his family.

★ ★ ★

As dusk fell, Jack snapped on the table lamp on the writing desk in his living room and opened Melanie's personnel file. He couldn't help a quick glance at the windows to make sure no one was watching. Although he had every right to check the personnel files of his staff, he still felt uncomfortable. Probably because if Melanie knew what he was doing, she'd be furious.

Since his faux pas over the wedding,

he'd spent more time with Melanie and he'd got to know her better. She didn't suffer fools gladly. Unfortunately, he had a nasty suspicion she now thought he was a bit of a fool. The assumption was completely wrong, of course, but she was not going to be easily won over. In fact, she seemed oblivious to his charms. He would have to work very hard to get back in her good books.

He flipped through her file, checking her past employment history. She'd joined his hotel staff a little over two months ago. Prior to that, she'd done various management jobs in the tourist industry. Up until five years ago, she'd been a receptionist and then practice manager for a doctors' surgery in Kent, where she'd worked for the first seven years after she left school. What had happened to make her change careers?

During the job interview, he vaguely remembered her telling him she'd lost her husband five years ago. He jotted the number of the doctors' surgery on a pad and put the note in his pocket. Maybe they would be able to give him more information.

He flipped over a page, and found a small headshot of her clipped inside the back cover of the folder. He tugged the photo free and held it under the light. The picture was a few years old, but she hadn't changed much; perhaps a few worry lines, but if she'd lost her husband that was understandable.

Her hair hung loose around her shoulders, longer than she wore it now, and gleaming with chestnut highlights. Her eyes, sometimes hazel, sometimes green depending on the light, were a rich mossy green in the photo. Why hadn't he realised how pretty she was when he first met her?

A knock on his front door dragged him out of his reverie. He sidled up to the living room window and took a peek at his visitor. Melanie stood there, arms wrapped around her ribs, glancing furtively over her shoulder.

Good gracious, what was she doing here now? He checked his watch. It was almost ten. Shouldn't she be at home with her son? He raced across the room and jammed the papers back into her personnel file then looked around for a hiding place for the folder and pushed it under the sofa seat and piled cushions on top of it so she didn't sit there.

Another knock sounded on the door, louder this time. 'Hold on. I'm coming.' Jack took a last look round the room, pulled the door open and smiled.

She pushed straight past him and moved into the shadows. 'You took your time. I thought someone would see me.'

'Would that be such a terrible thing?' he asked, slightly miffed. 'Surely being associated with me isn't that awful?'

'That's not the point and you know it.' She paced further into the room and glanced around. A flash of alarm shot through Jack as her perusal focused on the sofa. When she turned back to him, he released his breath.

'You certainly opened a can of worms when you made your rash comment to Stephanie about loving me.'

'I'm aware of that.' He wondered how he could make this up to her. 'Is there one worm in particular you're referring to?'

Melanie paced away and to his horror dropped down on the sofa. Most of the cushions he'd carefully arranged a moment earlier bounced on to the floor. Distractedly, she picked one up and hugged it. 'Your mother came to see me today — not that I'm calling your mother a worm.'

'Oh, heck.' His mother could certainly exhibit worm-like qualities when she wanted to. 'What has she heard?'

'Sounds as though she's been talking to Stephanie.'

'Was she angry?'

'Not angry, exactly . . . '

'Hang on a tick.' Jack strode through to the kitchen and poured himself a glass of Pinot Grigio. He needed fortification before he discussed his mother. 'Want a glass of wine?' he shouted through to the living room.

'I don't drink.'

'What, never?' Jack asked as he walked back to join her.

'No.' Her uncompromising tone sent up a red flag in his mind. He'd have to remember her aversion to alcohol. He glanced at his cold glass of Dutch courage and reluctantly placed it on the table untouched.

'Actually, your mother invited me to Sunday dinner.'

'Did she now?' Jack had expected his mother to be furious about the aborted wedding after she had worked so hard to persuade him to marry Stephanie. What was the woman up to now? She was always up to something.

'She wants us to get married,' Melanie said distractedly.

He clenched his fist against his thigh. After their lunch in the pub he'd realised he really liked Melanie but he planned to take things slowly, give her a chance to get to know him before he asked her out. He didn't want his mother interfering.

Melanie stood and Jack watched anxiously as the sofa cushions bounced. 'In fact, she tried to blackmail me.'

'She what?' Jack snatched up his glass without thinking and took a gulp. 'How?'

'She said she owns twenty-five percent of the hotel, and if I don't come to dinner on Sunday I'll lose my job.'

'She has no right.' Jack finished his glass of wine in a couple of swigs and sat on the seat over Melanie's personnel file. He couldn't take any more shocks tonight.

'That's what I thought.' Melanie came and stood in front of him, so close he could smell her powdery fragrance. He suspected it was baby powder or something to do with her son, but, crazy as it seemed, it still made his pulse-rate jump when it was on her. 'If she only holds twenty-five percent she can't force you to sack me — so I won't go to her dinner.'

Jack grimaced and rubbed the back of his neck. 'Actually, if she suddenly wanted her investment back that might prove awkward. Not that the money isn't there, it's just tied up.'

'So she could make you sack me.' Melanie sat down beside him and rested her head back on the sofa. Their bodies almost touched. It was the closest Jack had ever been to her, and they were alone in the darkened room. He eased nearer, just a fraction so she wouldn't notice, and reached for her hand. Miraculously, she let him touch her without pulling away.

'Why don't you come to the family lunch with me on Sunday? The food will be good and you'll like my cousins. Emily's married with two boys; Sam's five and Mathew's seven. Pippa's pregnant and not married so we don't talk about that. And Uncle Bernie is okay; a male version of Mother, but toned down to acceptable levels.'

Gently he slid his fingers around Melanie's hand and held it properly.

She turned her head and looked at him. The subdued light illuminated the pearly gloss on her lips. She had full lips and he imagined how soft they would feel when he kissed her.

'What about Ryan?'

Jack felt rotten for thinking about what he wanted when she was worried about her son. 'Bring him along too. He can play with Sam and Matt. He'll have a great time. You never know, when Mother finds out you have a son, she might lose interest in you as a prospective daughter-in-law.'

'Do you think so?' She brightened slightly, making Jack feel even worse. He had a nasty suspicion his mother would love a ready-made grandchild.

'I'm looking forward to meeting Ryan. You've been here for two months, and I've never been introduced to him.'

Melanie's smile dropped away, and she pulled her hand out of his grip. 'I must go. Sheila, the handyman's wife, is keeping an eye on Ryan for me for half-an-hour.'

Jack watched her as she ran across his back garden so she wouldn't be seen leaving his house. She was so neat and controlled; she even ran in small economical strides, her arms tight to her sides. He longed to muss her up, make her forget herself. She squeezed through a gap in the hedge that led to the manager's flat in the loft of what used to be the stables.

From his upstairs bathroom window, he occasionally saw Ryan playing in the small fenced grassy area near the old stables. Melanie never brought her son into the hotel, preferring to use the private entrance to her flat from the road. It hadn't bothered Jack before, but now he wondered why she was so secretive. Why did she keep the boy away from the hotel, and from him? It was almost as if she didn't want them to meet.

He pulled the crumpled file out from

under the sofa seat cushion and smoothed it flat. Melanie Marshall was a puzzle. Even if she had lost her husband, surely five years was long enough to mourn and start dating again. He opened the file and looked for her photo. When he didn't find it, he checked beneath the sofa cushion and with a sigh of relief, finally located the photo on the floor, half under the sofa. He must have dropped it in his haste to hide the file. Thank goodness Melanie hadn't found it in his house. That would have taken some explaining.

He smiled to himself. His mother's interference normally caused him trouble but she had done him a favour by persuading Melanie to come to dinner on Sunday. He just hoped his family didn't scare her off.

The phone was ringing as Melanie dashed in at her front door after seeing Jack. 'Thank you so much for watching Ryan,' she said to Sheila. 'Is everything all right?'

'He's still asleep. Good as gold, that boy is.' The older woman smiled to acknowledge Melanie's thanks and slipped out the door as the answering machine cut in.

Years of caution made Melanie stand over the phone waiting to see who was calling so late. She only picked up the receiver when she heard her grandmother's voice.

'Grandma, are you all right?' she asked with concern.

Her grandmother's weary sigh hissed down the line. 'I'm sorry to ring so late, dear. Your mother's been on the phone again this evening pressing me to give her your number.'

'You didn't tell her, did you?'

'No, dear. But I can't keep putting them off. You'll have to ring your mum and dad sometime. They want to see Ryan.'

Melanie shook her head and closed her eyes as her chest tightened with a swirl of painful emotion. 'No!'

Instead of supporting her in her hour

of need, her parents had turned their backs on her when the people of Littlechurch unjustly tarred her with the same brush as her larcenous husband. If it hadn't been for her grandma, she'd have had nobody to turn to for help. Her parents hadn't even bothered to visit Ryan when he was in hospital. As far as she was concerned, they had forfeited their right to a grandchild after the way they behaved.

'You'll have to talk to them eventually, dear,' her grandmother said.

Melanie released a fraught breath. It wasn't fair to expect her grandma to play gatekeeper for her, but she just could not bring herself to speak to her mother.

'They started it,' she said tightly. 'They were the ones who stopped speaking to me.'

'I know, pet, but you must try to see things from their point of view.' Melanie zoned out as her grandmother launched into the familiar excuse that because her parents owned the pub in Littlechurch they'd been frightened that if they went against public opinion they would lose their customers.

Her parents had put their business interests above the welfare of their own daughter and grandson and she would never forgive them.

3

On the dot of eleven on Sunday morning, Melanie saw Jack's Mercedes pull up in the road outside her flat.

She locked the front door behind her and negotiated her way down the steps, Ryan's hand tightly clasped in her own hand, his car seat in her other.

Jack was out of his car and heading for the steps, hastening to relieve her of the child seat. 'You were quick coming out.'

'Hmm.' Melanie smiled. 'I didn't want to keep you waiting.' She also didn't want him inside her flat. Although she'd been inside his house and was being press-ganged into Sunday lunch with his family, she still wanted to keep their personal lives as separate as possible. She had the terrible sensation that events were running out of control. If she wasn't careful, Stephanie's gossip about Melanie and Jack being an item might end up becoming reality.

'I thought this visit would require Sunday best?' Melanie eyed the faded denim jeans hugging Jack's lower body in all the right places.

'I always play football with the boys after lunch.'

'Football!' Ryan, shy and subdued since they left the flat, jumped up and down, hanging on Melanie's hand. 'Can I play?'

'Of course.' Jack squatted in front of Ryan and held out his hand. 'I'm Jack. You must be Ryan. Pleased to meet you.'

Solemnly, Ryan put his small hand in Jack's and shook. 'Pleased to meet you. Mum said I must call you Mr Summers.'

Jack grunted derisively. 'Mr Summers is my dad. You can call me Jack.'

Ryan giggled. This was exactly what Melanie had feared. They'd been in Jack's company for only a few minutes

58

and already he was wheedling his way into her son's affections.

In a rush of efficiency, she swept Ryan towards the car. 'In you pop, now. We don't want to keep Mr Summers's mother waiting, do we?'

With his eyes self-consciously on Jack, Ryan made a show of settling himself in his seat. When Melanie tried to fasten the straps, he pushed her hands away. 'I want to do it.'

'I need to check it's done properly, Ryan. Be a good boy.'

Jack, who'd seated himself, looked over his shoulder. 'Let your mum check the straps, Ryan, or we'll never get any lunch. Aren't you hungry?'

When Ryan immediately moved his hands and let her fasten his seatbelt, a burst of anger burned through Melanie. She could look after her son herself; she did not need a man interfering. She marched around the car, climbed in and slammed the door.

Jack raised his eyebrows as he started the engine. She leaned towards him and whispered vehemently, 'I want your word you won't interfere again when I'm dealing with my son, or we get out of this car now.'

His expression tightened. 'I'm driving; it's my responsibility to make sure anyone under fourteen is properly strapped in. Check your highway code if you don't believe me.'

Mortified, Melanie bit her lip. Jack was just being a responsible driver. After the way her husband had behaved, she of all people should applaud that. Heat flushed into her face. 'Sorry. I hadn't thought of it that way.'

'Of course you hadn't. You're so busy trying to keep me at a distance, you can't think of anything else.' His jaw clenched as he slammed the gear lever into first and pulled away. An uncomfortable silence filled the car.

Melanie stared out of her side window, the tiny hairs on her neck prickling with the tension. Why was he so bothered by her wish to keep to herself? He'd been happy with the way she behaved before he left for Barbados. Surely he'd be relieved to put all this fake relationship nonsense behind them and get back to normal.

Jack didn't say another word until they turned between two granite pillars and followed a long driveway flanked by rambling rhododendron bushes. 'This is Hazelwood House.' He swung the car around a circular patch of gravel and parked beside a black four-wheel drive.

Grand was the first word that came to mind when she stared at the magnificent Georgian manor. It looked nearly as large as Jack's hotel.

Jack was already out of the car and holding her door open by the time Melanie moved. Without looking at her, he waited with his hands in the pockets of his jeans while she helped Ryan from his seat.

A brooding young Italian man, wearing impossibly tight black trousers and a blue silk shirt, opened the front door.

'Marco,' Jack said nodding. 'This is Melanie.'

Marco scanned her with a lazy appraisal that made her feel uncomfortable. There was something sleazy about him. He held out his hand but she really did not want to touch him and after the handshake, she rubbed her palm on her trousers.

'Who is he?' she whispered to Jack as she watched Marco sauntered away.

'My mother's toy boy.'

'Her what?' Melanie's eyes widened in horror.

'He keeps her happy for the moment. I think she's trying to keep up with my father.'

Jack indicated Melanie should follow Marco. She took Ryan's hand and led him down the hallway, Jack behind her.

Although Melanie had viewed the meal as a trial, once they were seated around a huge oval table in the dining room, the lunch actually turned out to be fun.

Jack was right; Melanie discovered

she liked his cousin Emily, and her two sons immediately made friends with Ryan. The three boys sat together at one end of the table chattering non-stop about television programmes, school and football.

Jack's pregnant cousin Pippa wore an air of aloof melancholy and spent most of the time talking softly to Marco. Melanie expected subtle — or not-so-subtle — pressure from Mrs Summers to discuss her relationship with Jack, but she was the perfect hostess. Jack still seemed annoyed with her, and although he sat beside her, he left her to talk to Emily and spent his time discussing share prices and the strength of the pound with his uncle.

As soon as the boys were given permission to leave the table after lunch, Sam and Matt raced out the French windows into the back garden with Ryan in tow as though he'd been friends with them all his life.

'Jack, Jack,' the boys chanted.

The adults all smiled indulgently, and

Jack gave a mock sigh. 'Duty calls.'

Emily slapped him on the arm as he walked past her towards the garden. 'You big kid.' She turned to Melanie. 'Don't fall for his act. He loves this as much as the boys do.'

Jack gave the first real smile Melanie had seen from him since their argument and headed out the French windows.

'Want to go and watch the show?' Emily asked.

Melanie agreed instantly; she was itching to go out and check on Ryan and, she couldn't deny, she was curious to see Jack playing football.

When she reached the garden, Jack had removed his jacket, rolled up his shirtsleeves and was bouncing a football on his toe with the precision of an expert. The three boys each had balls and were trying to imitate his trick without success.

Melanie felt her mouth fall open as Jack flicked the ball up, caught it behind his back on his heel, flicked it forward onto his toe again, then repeated the move.

'You're impressed.' The hint of amusement in Emily's voice made Melanie snap her mouth shut. 'I take it you don't know his history, then?'

'What history?'

Emily indicated the swing seat under an oak tree and they sat together to watch as they chatted.

'Jack started his career as a professional footballer straight out of school. He was the golden boy — captain of the school team, played for his county, headhunted by one of the big-name teams. Unfortunately, it all came to a sad end. After a few years, his knees couldn't take the punishment and he had to give up. Football was his world, and for a while, I thought losing that would finish him.'

Emily paused and shook her head. Melanie put her hand over her mouth. A professional footballer? If someone had told her Jack was an alien, she couldn't be more surprised. She looked at him manipulating the ball effortlessly. Now she knew his history, the well-developed leg muscles of a sportsman were obvious beneath the tight denim of his jeans.

'What did he do after that?' she asked.

'It gets worse.' Emily grimaced. 'His fiancée left him standing at the altar a few weeks later. Jack really needed his father's support, but Francis Summers chose that moment to walk out on Imelda. Jack's dad always let him down, but this was the final straw. I don't think Jack's spoken to him since.'

'Oh.' It was all Melanie could say. When she told Jack they didn't know each other, she had no idea just how little she knew of him. 'Where's Jack's father now?'

'New York, shacked up with his latest bimbo.' Emily nodded towards Marco, who was leaning against the wall, sulkily smoking a cigarette. 'Imelda's trying to beat Francis at his own game. She wants someone to love her, but she's looking in the wrong place. Marco just likes spending her money. I think that's why she's so keen for Jack to marry and give her grandchildren to dote on.'

Pity and just a touch of guilt stole through Melanie. If Imelda hoped she would marry Jack and provide the grandchildren she so badly wanted, she would be disappointed.

Once the boys tired of the tricks, Jack set up a goal between two plant pots and let them try to kick balls past him. Melanie held her breath every time he threw himself to the ground, worried he'd hurt himself. He cleverly missed the strikes without making it obvious, letting each boy score a goal every few kicks, much to their delight.

Melanie was so in awe of Jack's athletic display, it wasn't until the game ended that she realised, with a little shiver of concern, that Ryan was equally star-struck. When Jack took a dive for the final ball and made sure he missed, all three boys jumped on him screaming. Ryan was right in there with the others, wrestling on the ground, eyes bright with excitement.

Emily crossed her arms and shook her head. 'The washing machine will be busy tonight. Why does male bonding always involve getting dirty?' She released a lingering breath. 'My boys adore Jack. He's so good with them. I wish their father took half the interest in them that Jack does.'

'Where is your husband?' Melanie hadn't liked to ask before Emily raised the subject herself.

'He's a commodity broker. Money's great, family life is rubbish. He's supposed to spend the week in London and come home for weekends, but lately he's forgotten we exist.' Emily looked at Melanie and bit her lip. 'I'm not sure if I'm speaking out of turn as it's so soon after Stephanie, but if you get the chance, hang on to Jack. He's a keeper.'

Before Melanie could answer, Emily leapt up and strode towards the heap of grass-stained arms and legs on the lawn. 'Come on now kids — all four of you,' she added, grinning at Jack as he disentangled himself.

Jack sat on the grass, his hair a mess, his clothes muddy and grass-stained, grinning down at Ryan in his lap. Ryan leaned back against Jack's chest and gave Melanie a contented smile.

She caught her breath with a sudden, almost painful yearning for a happy settled family life, for a man like Jack to love her and Ryan ... but it was something she knew she could never have.

* * *

The following week, the comfortable professional relationship Melanie had established with Jack before he left for Barbados became a distant memory. Everywhere Melanie went, Jack seemed to be, and simply being in the same room with him set her nerves jangling with awareness as if he exuded some sort of force field.

On Friday afternoon, unable to cope

with the assault on her senses, Melanie hid away in the cellar on the pretext of looking for invoices the accountant had requested. The boiler hummed beside her, making the room unbearably hot as she searched through dusty boxes of old business documents.

Sweat and dust prickled her skin as she checked her watch for the millionth time. With a spurt of relief, she realised she only had fifteen minutes left before she could escape to collect Ryan from school.

She wiped the back of her hand across her forehead. This situation was ridiculous. How could she be reduced to hiding from her boss? Why wasn't Jack out pursuing business opportunities for the hotel so she didn't keep tripping over him?

As if summoned by her thoughts, Jack appeared at the door and sauntered down the narrow stairs. The harsh light from the bare bulb sculpted his face into an exquisite masterpiece of light and shadow. Her heart did a crazy somersault and she concentrated on her hands.

'Is it my imagination, or are you avoiding me?' he asked.

'I'm not,' she fired back without looking at him.

'We need to talk about what's going on between us.'

She made a show of riffling through the box of papers, although her mind had blanked the moment she became aware of him watching her.

'There is no 'us'. I told you before we came to lunch on Sunday that it didn't mean anything.'

He took a step closer. 'I'm not talking about lunch,' he said, with a touch of exasperation in his tone. 'Steph noticed that we have chemistry and I feel it myself. You must admit there's something between us.'

'I don't want to talk about what Stephanie thinks.' Melanie closed her eyes and bit her lip. Why was he interested in her? Why couldn't he turn his charm onto someone else and leave her to do her job?

Moving a few steps closer, he blocked her view of the door. 'Melanie. Look at me.'

She kept her gaze fixed on the box of documents, terrified that if he saw her face he'd see into her heart. His inquisitive blue gaze would penetrate beneath the brisk businesslike persona that she used to keep people at a distance and he'd discover her secrets. She couldn't risk getting close to him. She couldn't bear to see the look of condemnation on his face if he discovered the truth about her past.

'I can't discuss this, Jack.'

He laid his hand over hers to still her busy fingers. 'Melanie,' he whispered, his tone low, compelling, sending a flutter of longing through her. 'Talk to me, please.'

He raised his other hand and his fingertips cradled her chin, gently turning her face up to his so she had to look at him.

Melanie closed her eyes in a hopeless

attempt to fight the temptation of his seductive charm. The pad of his thumb grazed the corner of her lips.

'Why fight this chemistry between us? Allow me to take you out on a proper date so we can get to know each other. You might even find you like me,' he added with a touch of self-deprecating humour.

'I won't date my boss,' she whispered desperately.

'Shall I sack you, then?'

Her eyes flew open. 'No, I . . . ' Trapped in the simmering blue heat in his eyes, her mind stalled. The heady scent of spicy soap and warm male skin sent heat rushing across her skin. 'I . . . I . . . ' Somewhere far away on the edge of her awareness the grandfather clock in the entrance hall above chimed three times. 'I have to collect Ryan.'

Snatching a breath, Melanie ducked under Jack's arm and stumbled up the narrow stairs, dragging herself up the handrail as though it were a lifeline. She dashed into the manager's office, terrified Jack would follow. Grabbing her handbag, she slipped out of her work shoes, then kicked them under the chair and stepped into her flats. As she headed for the front door, Jack emerged from the hall that led to the cellar.

Breath coming in uneven snatches — more to do with what happened in the cellar than the speed of her stride — she tried to focus on meeting Ryan and calm down. This was crazy behaviour. She was thirty, not sixteen.

After her dash down the street, she reached the school ten minutes early and had to wait. Leaning against the green metal railings outside the flat-roofed building of the infants' classrooms, she massaged her temples.

How could she continue to work with Jack now? When she looked at him she wanted to see the charming, politely aloof man who'd employed her, but his attitude to her had changed.

He smiled at her as if he knew what she was thinking. He touched her whenever he could, a casual brush of fingers on her sleeve or a polite hand to her back as they passed through a door — maddening moments of contact that ought to mean nothing but which made her brain turn to fluff and her skin burn.

And every time she looked at him, she remembered him flopped on the lawn after playing football with the kids, his hair mussed, his eyes sparkling, and Ryan happily cradled in his lap.

Jack was ruining all her plans.

'Mrs Marshall?'

Melanie looked up, startled by the sound of her name.

Ryan's form teacher stood on the pavement in front of her, smiling, while Ryan chatted happily to his friend close by.

'I understand congratulations are in order,' she said.

Congratulations? Melanie racked her befuddled brain to try to remember if she'd entered a draw run by the parents' association or something and came up blank.

'I'm sorry, I'm not with you?' She shook her head.

'Your impending nuptials.'

'My *what?*'

'Ryan told me today that Jack Summers is going to be his new daddy. It's not a secret, is it?'

'He what?' The mild ache in Melanie's temples pounded with her heartbeat as she glanced at her son's happy smile. 'I'm afraid Ryan's confused. Jack's just my boss.'

The teacher frowned, then smiled apologetically. 'I'm sorry. I just assumed after the story I heard about Mr Summers's break up with that solicitor . . . Never mind. Must be a case of wishful thinking on Ryan's part.'

'Yes.' Melanie nodded as Ryan skipped towards her, grinning. 'Wishful thinking.'

Her chest tightened with doubts as Ryan looked up at her, brown eyes sparkling with excitement. Surely Ryan was only dazzled by Jack's skill with a football. If she kept Ryan away from

Jack and distracted him with other things, her son would soon forget his obsession.

'Did you have a good day at school?' she asked her son with forced brightness.

He jumped up and down. 'Can we see Jack tonight?'

Melanie glanced away and counted to three. 'Not tonight, darling. We're going to get your feet measured. Maybe you can have new shoes.'

'New shoes. New shoes,' Ryan chanted as they set off along the pavement towards the shops. At least she'd turned his attention away from Jack.

'Can I go and show Jack my new shoes?'

'No!' Melanie snapped before she could stop herself. 'No, sweetheart,' she added gently. 'Jack will be having his tea.'

'Can we have tea with him?'

'He hasn't invited us.'

'We can invite him to our house, then.'

'Not tonight.'

'When?' Ryan pulled on her hand. 'When can he come, Mummy? I want to play football again.'

As Ryan's demands became more insistent, Melanie's insides wound tighter. She had to get off the pavement, away from the people pushing past them, or she was going to scream.

Melanie guided Ryan to a wooden bench beneath a willow tree in the nearby park and they sat. 'Look, sweetheart. You can't tell people Jack is going to be your daddy when he isn't.'

'But he's your boyfriend. That makes him nearly my daddy.'

'He's not my boyfriend. I work with him.'

Swinging his legs, Ryan looked down and twisted the hem of his tee shirt. 'My friend Martin says Jack dumped his mum's friend because he wants to marry you.'

Melanie briefly covered her eyes. So the gossip had reached the playground. 'Dumped isn't a nice word, Ryan,' she said, evading the topic.

Ryan's little legs stilled and he looked up at her, his face creased with concentration. 'If I tell Jack I want him to be my dad, will he marry you then?'

A knot cinched tight around Melanie's heart and she couldn't catch her breath. She'd been so sure the way to protect Ryan from being hurt again was to raise him alone. She would not let her parents back into his life just so they could reject him again and she would never give another man the chance to get close.

But she'd ignored the fact he might need a man's company. In trying to protect him, had she instead deprived him of something important?

A little boy's voice rang out from the playground on the other side of the park, calling for his dad. Melanie stared at the children scrambling across a wooden climbing frame, at the mums and dads standing together ready to lend a helping hand. Their brightly coloured clothes fractured into a kaleidoscope of colour through her tears. She blinked rapidly and swallowed.

Had she deluded herself? Who was she really protecting? Had she sacrificed Ryan's happiness to guard her own heart? How could she have been so blind, so selfish?

If it hadn't been for Jack, she might have cut Ryan off from adult male company until he was a teenager. She needed to do some serious thinking, reassess her priorities. Whatever it took, she must do what was best for her son.

4

After Melanie left the hotel, Jack paced back and forth across his office. If he didn't know why she refused to date, how would he ever overcome her objections? Yet every time he tried to talk to her about how he felt, she changed the subject or ran away. He guessed some man had really done a number on her. Top of the list of suspects was her husband. The man may be dead, but he certainly was not forgotten.

He should ask Melanie about her past and let her decide how much she wanted to reveal. The trouble was that she was so secretive, he suspected she wouldn't tell him a darn thing.

He fished out of his pocket the note of the doctors' surgery telephone number and stared at it. His conscience squirmed at the thought of checking on her behind her back, but what other option did he have?

Decision made, the tension in his neck eased. He strode around the desk, snatched up the phone and started to dial. At the last minute, he slammed the handset down. He couldn't call from the hotel line. Knowing how efficient Melanie was, she'd be bound to spot the telephone number of where she used to work listed on the itemised phone bill. He rubbed the back of his neck thoughtfully. He'd have to use his home phone.

A few minutes later, he walked through his front door. He fixed himself a stiff drink — almost unheard-of for him mid-afternoon, but he thought he'd earned it after the week he'd had. He sat at the writing desk in his living room and dialled the doctors' surgery in Kent where Melanie had worked.

'Good afternoon, Littlechurch surgery, can I help you?' a brightly efficient female voice answered.

'I need some information on a

woman who used to work at the surgery.'

There was silence on the other end of the line for a few seconds. 'We're not allowed to give out details like that.'

'I'm an employer. The surgery was quoted as a reference.'

'Oh, I see. Let me put you through to the practice manager. Can I have your name please?'

Jack baulked a bit at this request. He'd hoped to remain anonymous so there was no chance his enquiry would get back to Melanie. Only after he'd given his real name did it occur to him that he could have used a false one.

'Good afternoon, Mr Summers. I'm the practice manager. Who were you wanting a reference for?'

'Melanie Marshall.'

A heavy silence descended on the other end of the line. When the woman spoke again, her tone was clipped. 'Mrs Marshall left our employ when her husband left the practice.'

'Her husband worked there as well?'

The silence deepened.

'Doctor Marshall was one of the partners.' She was quiet for so long, Jack thought they'd been cut off then in a warning tone she added, 'Before you employ Mrs Marshall, I strongly advise you to do some research on the Internet. That's all I'm willing to say over the phone. If you want anything more, please put your request in writing. Goodbye.'

The dialling tone hummed in his ear and he frowned. Search on the Internet for what — Melanie's name? Was she famous? He'd never heard of her before, although the name Doctor Marshall rang a bell somewhere in the back of his mind. A chill crept through him.

Jack opened his laptop, turned it until he got a signal from the wireless router in the hotel, and typed 'Doctor Marshall' into a search engine. A page of results popped up, but before Jack had a chance to scan them, a knock sounded.

He gazed at the front door warily; he'd be willing to bet that his visitor was Melanie. She had a habit of catching him out. This time he'd be prepared. He closed the page and shut the lid on his laptop before he headed for the door. Through the small diamond-shaped glass panel, he saw chestnut hair and he smiled to himself in anticipation of seeing her.

When Jack opened the door, he found Ryan beside her, drumming his feet on the path. 'Look at my new shoes,' the boy burst out with obvious glee.

Jack smiled and ruffled Ryan's short dark hair. 'Wow, they're super smart.' He turned his attention to Melanie and his smile faded. Her eyes were red as though she'd been crying. 'What . . . ?' Instinctively, he raised his arm to hug her but then let it fall back to his side. Frustration warred with concern. She'd run from his touch earlier so he couldn't risk touching her again, even to give her comfort. He stepped aside. 'Come on in.'

Ryan belted in and started picking things up, exploring his new surroundings. 'Look with your eyes, not your hands, Ryan,' Melanie warned, although her voice lacked its usual ring of authority. She sounded weary and defeated.

'Would you like a cup of tea?' he asked.

'We need to talk.'

He felt like saying he'd been trying to talk to her all week and she'd avoided him, but she obviously wasn't in the mood to appreciate the irony.

'Let's talk while we have some tea. Do you want to go out in the garden, Ryan?'

The boy scampered towards the back door and hauled on the handle. Jack helped him open it and watched as he raced outside. Melanie followed Ryan out and glanced around. 'Stay on the lawn where I can see you, sweetheart,' she said.

Jack carried their cups of tea outside. The two of them sat on a bench facing the garden and watched Ryan run around in circles looking down at his new shoes.

'Life's so simple when you're young, isn't it?' Jack said.

'Hmm.' Melanie wrapped her hands around her cup and sipped. 'I've been thinking.' He stilled, sensing this was important. 'I'm sorry I've avoided you this week; it's just that I've been confused.'

'I'm a bit confused myself,' he quipped, trying to lighten her mood. She gave no response.

'I'm not ready for any sort of romantic relationship.'

Jack's chest tightened and he quashed his instinct to try to persuade her otherwise. He sensed a 'but' coming.

'What I would like is a friend.' She curled her lips into a smile and it looked like an effort. His arms ached to pull her into the safety of his embrace, protect her from whatever had caused her pain and made her cry. 'Since the accident that killed my husband and injured Ryan, I've been a little over-protective.' She took another sip of tea and her hands trembled around the cup. 'And I now think that's been a mistake.'

Jack suppressed his burst of relief that she might confide in him and kept his voice level. 'Is that how Ryan got his scars?'

'You've noticed them.' She pulled out a tissue from her bag and wiped her nose.

'What happened?' he asked gently, hoping she'd open up and give him an insight into her problems.

For long moments, she stared silently into the lengthening shadows. 'It's a long story. The crux of it is that my husband was drunk so I told him not to take Ryan out in the car, but he ignored me. The rest is history . . . he lost control, and my little boy nearly lost his arm . . . I swore I'd never trust a man with Ryan's safety again.' She looked down and wiped her nose.

After a few moments, Jack realised that was all the explanation he'd get for now. It was a start. Gradually, one step at a time, he'd convince her to trust him. 'So now you've had a re-think?' he prompted.

'Watching you play with him last Sunday made me realise he needs the influence of a man in his life.'

'A role model,' Jack added, remembering how he'd longed for his own father to take an interest in him when he was young.

'Perhaps.' She smiled again, and he was pleased to see that this time it reached her eyes. 'He idolises you, Jack. He told his teacher today that you were going to be his new dad . . . '

'Did he now?' Interesting, he thought.

Ryan had stopped running in circles and was springing around like a kangaroo, still looking at his new shoes. Jack sympathised with the boy for wanting a father. It was no fun going to watch a football match with your mother — he remembered the experience vividly. Although with the benefit of hindsight, he appreciated how much effort Imelda had made to compensate for his father's disinterest.

Jack loved kids. He just seemed to click with them, especially little boys who enjoyed football. Maybe Ryan would turn out to be his strongest ally in winning Melanie's heart.

'So what do you mean by friends?' he asked.

Melanie sat up straighter and flicked back her hair. 'Perhaps you could play football with Ryan and be there for him when he needs a man to talk to . . . '

'That's no problem.'

'Maybe come out with us some-times . . . '

Jack fought to keep the smile from his face. This was starting to sound promising. The more time he spent with Melanie, the more chance he had to prove to her that she could trust him.

'Any time you want to go out, just let me know,' he told her.

She fiddled with the strap on her handbag. 'There's one thing that bothers me . . . you won't drop Ryan when you get another girlfriend, will you?'

He clenched his jaw and some of his hope filtered away. Melanie seemed determined to ignore the fact he was interested in her as well. But all he said was, 'I won't let him down. I promise.'

'Good.' She smiled properly, her eyes glowing in a way that made her whole face light up. She checked her watch. 'I must make Ryan some tea before he flakes out on me.'

'Why don't you leave him here, go home and cook while I fetch a ball? Ryan and I can have a knock around in my garden until you're ready for him.'

Melanie jumped up and hooked her bag over her shoulder. 'You're sure you don't mind?'

Jack stood, linked his fingers behind his neck and stretched his tense shoulders. 'Believe me, the exercise will do me good.'

Her eyes flicked over him, and he thought there might be a spark of female appreciation there before she averted her gaze.

'Okay.' She took a step closer, rested her fingers lightly on his shoulder and gave him a peck on the check. 'Thanks, Jack.'

She was half way across the garden before he recovered from the shock of what had just happened.

She'd touched him, kissed him no less, with no prompting! He put his hand to his cheek; the kiss had been a fleeting brush of her lips, but the spot still tingled. He must be doing something right for a change. He watched until she squeezed through the gap in the hedge before he headed inside to find a ball.

On his way past his laptop, he made a decision. He wouldn't pry into her past. He'd wait until she was ready to tell him what the scandal was that the doctors' surgery had hinted at. If he wanted her to trust him, he must trust her as well.

★   ★   ★

A few weeks later, Melanie looked up from preparing lunch at the sound of footfalls on the steps outside her flat. Jack appeared in the open doorway and leaned a shoulder against the door frame.

'Lovely day,' he said.

'It certainly is. Summer's well and truly here.'

In fact, it had been a lovely three weeks, both weather-wise and in other ways. Jack had been wonderful, always ready to spend time with Ryan after school when he wanted to play outside. Jack had also been the perfect gentleman. After their talk, he'd backed off. With the pressure for a romantic relationship lifted, they were much closer. Although she still found herself aware of Jack in a way she hadn't been before, she put it down to the fact that she knew him better and was therefore more in tune with him.

'Where's Ryan?' Jack glanced around the small living room.

'Drawing, last time I checked.'

Melanie turned off the heat under her cheese sauce and went to Ryan's bedroom door. 'Jack's here, sweetheart.'

Ryan dropped his crayon and leaped to his feet. 'Jack!' He belted towards the front door and hugged Jack's legs.

Melanie tightened her grip on the smooth wooden handle of her spoon and went back to stirring her sauce. Sometimes she felt like a voyeur watching the two of them together. As though she were an outsider peeping in on a world she could never be a part of.

'Come across to my garden for a few minutes,' Jack said to Ryan. 'Mum as well,' he added looking up at Melanie. 'I've got something to show you.'

Ryan swung on Jack's arm as Melanie followed them down the steps. After a short walk across the old cobbled stable yard, they pushed between the hedging shrubs into Jack's back garden. Ryan went through first and squealed with excitement, pricking Melanie's curiosity to see what was there.

On the square of lawn flanked by curved rainbows of flowerbeds stood a trampoline. Jack pushed aside the blue safety netting enclosing it and heaved Ryan onto the bouncing surface. Kicking off his shoes and socks, Jack followed Ryan up. Melanie crossed her arms and smiled as Jack took Ryan's hands and they jumped together.

'Look, Mummy, look.'

Melanie waved. 'Wow, look at you bouncing high.'

'Come on too, Mummy.'

'I don't think it's a Mummy sort of thing, sweetheart.'

Jack grinned at her. 'Nonsense. Up you come.' Jack pushed aside the safety netting and offered his hand.

Melanie looked down at her skirt and blouse. 'I'm not dressed for it.'

The corner of Jack's mouth quirked up. 'We'll wait while you go and put on your leotard, then.'

She couldn't help grinning back at him as he waited, hand still held ready to help her up. 'Oh, all right.' She toed off her shoes. 'But just for a few minutes.'

Very conscious of Jack standing above her, she leaned her knee on the edge, being careful not to expose too much thigh. Jack's large, warm hand enclosed hers and, as he hauled her up, Ryan chose that moment to plop onto his bottom. The rebound of the trampoline caught her off balance, and with a surprised squeak, she found herself propelled towards Jack. His arms closed around her, holding her fast against a chest that was every bit as hard and muscular as she'd expect of a professional sportsman.

Melanie closed her eyes as a thrill shivered down her spine, then simmered in the pit of her stomach. Torn between putting some distance between them and the fear of being dumped unceremoniously on her bottom and showing off her practical cotton knickers, she froze in the safety of Jack's arms. He didn't seem to have any trouble keeping his balance.

'Stay still a moment, Ryan.' Jack's voice sounded a little gruff, but it could be because she had her ear pressed against his chest. 'Let your mum find her feet.'

Once the surface beneath her stopped undulating, Jack loosened his arms and Melanie stepped away. She avoided his gaze, looking down at his bare feet instead. His toes were long and a little battered and her heart gave an odd little jump; even Jack had imperfections.

'Come on, everyone bounce together,' Jack said, grabbing her hand again.

Ryan took her other hand and they started to jump in time, but ended up out of sync. They tumbled down. Melanie landed on her back, Ryan across her legs, and Jack beside her. Ryan bounded up and launched himself at Jack who grunted as a small knee made contact with his belly. Melanie laughed so hard that tears ran down her cheeks.

Finally, the laughter subsided to chuckles and she lay still, an unfamiliar sense of contentment settling over her.

Jack held an excited Ryan at bay for a moment and smiled at her, the glint of boyish mischief in his eyes filling her head with very adult thoughts. She put a hand over her heart. It must be the bouncing that made it difficult to catch her breath.

'You shouldn't have done this, you know,' she said. 'You don't have to buy Ryan things.'

'What do you mean, 'buy Ryan things'? I've always wanted a trampoline, you know!'

'You really are just a kid at heart, aren't you?' After the words left her mouth, she flushed, hoping he wouldn't take it as an insult. He held her gaze for a moment, a smile playing around his lips, before turning his attention back to Ryan. Melanie smoothed down her skirt, crawled to the trampoline's edge then slid off.

'Will you get us a drink, please?' Jack shouted. 'There should be some in the fridge.'

Melanie collected some sodas from

Jack's kitchen and returned to the garden. Man and boy had given up wrestling and were sitting in the middle of the trampoline, engrossed in the male-bonding ritual of comparing scars, for which Jack had rolled up his trouser legs.

She paused to admire well-muscled calves dusted with golden hairs. Then she saw the scars on his knees.

Ryan ran his fingers across Jack's scars, his small face creased in concentration. 'Football did this to you?'

'Lots and lots of football, and not enough care.' Jack ruffled Ryan's hair. 'The sort of football you play won't hurt your knees, kiddo. Just remember, when Mummy tells you to stop doing something in case you hurt yourself, it's a good idea to listen. My mum told me to be careful, but I didn't take enough notice.'

'Want to see my scars?' Ryan asked.

Melanie's mouth fell open in surprise as Ryan pulled his shirt off over his head and exposed his shoulder. He was usually shy about the marks that ran down his neck and across his collarbone and shoulder. 'I was in a car accident. I was only one,' he said, almost proudly.

'Were you now?' Jack patted Ryan's shoulder. 'It looks like you must have been a very brave boy.'

'I was. Mummy said my arm nearly fell off.'

Melanie's fingers jerked reflexively and she nearly dropped the sodas. 'I never said anything of the sort, young man.'

'You did! I heard you tell Great Nana.'

Jack slanted her a sardonic glance then turned Ryan's shirt the right way out and pulled it over his head. 'You've got big ears for such a little chap. Look at them. Ryan's ears are so big his shirt won't fit over them.' At Jack's teasing, Ryan dissolved into giggles.

As she handed over the drink cans, Melanie gave Jack a grateful smile for distracting Ryan from memories of his injuries. He'd had nightmares for years after the accident. Normally, he didn't like to talk about his scars, although there'd been a touch of bravado in his voice when he'd shown them to Jack.

Jack jumped off the trampoline and Melanie tried not to notice the flash of hard abdominal muscle as he straightened his shirt and tucked it in.

'Ryan and I should go and have our lunch,' Melanie said.

'Hang on a moment. I've got something to show you.' Jack jogged into the house and returned thirty seconds later with a card in his hand. Without comment, he handed it to her.

She examined what turned out to be a wedding invitation. 'This is from your pregnant cousin Pippa, isn't it?'

'Yep. The baby's father found out she was pregnant. Apparently, he's Marco's cousin. He and Pip met when he was over visiting Marco. Mother says he turned up a few weeks ago and virtually dragged Pip back to Italy with him.'

'The wedding's in Positano. Lucky you. I've always wanted to visit the Amalfi coast. I hope you have a lovely time.'

'Come with me,' he said softly.

A flash of surprise tinged with longing caught her unawares. Of course, the feeling was purely because she wanted to visit Positano. The fact she'd be going with Jack had nothing to do with it. Melanie scanned his face, trying to fathom his intentions. So far, he'd honoured her wish to keep their relationship on a friendly footing. Could she trust him to be a gentleman if they went away together?

He smiled back, his expression unreadable.

'Ryan's school holiday will have started,' she said.

'We'd only be away for a few days. Haven't you any family he can stay with?'

'He could stay with my grandma. She

offered to have him for a week in the holidays.'

'That's settled, then.' He reached for the invitation.

She hung on to the card as his fingers closed around it. 'Jack . . . just friends, remember . . . ?'

'How could I forget?' he said, a touch sharply. 'The invitation says plus guest. I don't want to go alone.' She released the invitation, and he turned it over in his hands. When he spoke again, he seemed to have regained his good mood. 'You've been working so hard recently that I just thought you deserved a break. It'll be fun.'

She was tempted, very tempted. She hadn't been on holiday since before Ryan was born, and even then they'd never gone abroad because her husband wouldn't go far from his medical practice. 'Okay,' she said.

Jack flashed a smile that caused a twinge deep in her chest. 'Great. It's a date.'

A date? Melanie hoped she hadn't

made a huge mistake. Jack appeared to have forgotten the nonsense about her stepping into Stephanie's shoes as a prospective fiancée. Would he still be content with friendship alone when they reached the romantic Amalfi coast?

5

Jack had hired a red Ferrari! When he collected the car outside Naples airport, Melanie tried to appear nonchalant while inside she bubbled with secret delight. She'd expected them to take a taxi from the airport to the hotel he'd booked in Positano.

She'd had six weeks to question her decision to accompany him to the wedding and the previous night she had nearly backed out. Not that he'd done anything to make her uncomfortable; in reality, he'd continued to be friendly in an almost brotherly fashion. What worried her were the things that happened between them in her dreams. Some mornings when she saw him in the hotel, she could hardly look him in the eye.

Luckily, the flight from London to Naples was short so she hadn't dozed.

The thought of having a risqué dream about him while he sat beside her sent tingles of embarrassment racing through her. What if she talked in her sleep? Goodness, it didn't bear thinking about!

When he opened the car door for her, she gave him a brisk smile of thanks and settled inside. The best way to maintain her distance was to be coolly detached — or at least strive to appear that way. As the sports car engine roared to life, a trickle of unease went through her and she cast Jack a nervous sideways glance. 'We'll be driving on the wrong side of narrow roads. I don't want to go too fast.'

Jack released a long-suffering breath. 'Didn't your mother ever tell you the surest way to dent a man's ego is to question his driving skills? I know you like to be in control, Mel, but be gentle with me. We're on holiday.'

'I didn't mean — '

'Don't worry. I'm used to it.'

Used to what? Melanie fastened her

seatbelt and looked at him. 'I don't try to control you. How could I? You're my boss.'

Jack cut her a sardonic sideways glance then pulled away.

Disquiet over Jack's words niggled her. Just because she liked to ensure things were done properly didn't make her a control freak. Unless she checked on people's work regularly, they often cut corners. Surely Jack was pleased she kept a close eye on the hotel — but not, she supposed, if he felt it was critical of him.

She watched the crazy traffic shoot every-which-way. Like everything else Jack did, he negotiated his way through the melee that was Naples and out towards the coast with consummate skill and she slowly relaxed.

As they drove along the winding road that hugged the cliffs above the sparkling azure Mediterranean, Jack lowered the convertible top and warm wind whipped through her hair.

He slowed as they passed through a

tiny village; small white and terracotta houses decorated with ceramic pots overflowing with flowers defied gravity as they clung to the side of the cliff.

The locals turned to glance at them as they passed and she noticed that many of the women gave Jack a second look. He steered with one hand, his other arm resting along the back of her seat.

'This isn't my first time driving a Ferrari, you know,' he said. 'I went through quite an extravagant list of fast cars in my misspent youth.'

Melanie watched Jack surreptitiously and tried to see him as other women did: wind-ruffled golden hair, dark glasses, open-necked shirt giving a peek of chest, muscular forearms effortlessly controlling the car. She could easily believe the gossip she'd heard about him being a bit of a playboy in his early twenties. Just when she thought she knew the different facets of Jack's character — businessman, sportsman, family man — he changed like a chameleon to suit his surroundings and she saw another side of him.

If she hadn't accompanied him to Italy, she was certain he wouldn't have been without female company for long. Thank goodness she'd decided to come. Her flash of relief was quickly muted by a little burst of anger at herself. She firmed her lips and concentrated on the beautiful scenery. She must keep her unruly thoughts in check. He was her boss and it was none of her business who he dated — as long as he kept his promise to be friends with Ryan.

When they reached Positano, Jack drew the car to a halt outside a huge old hotel overlooking the sea. On the front, green wooden shutters were pinned open against pink plaster walls and beneath hung window boxes overflowing with scarlet geraniums. As Jack carried their bags inside, Melanie followed biting her lip anxiously; she'd trusted Jack to book the rooms and prayed she wouldn't discover he'd accidentally booked for them to share. She released a sigh of relief as the receptionist handed Jack two keys. It turned out their rooms weren't even on the same floor.

Alone in her room, she unpacked and hung the dress she'd bought to wear to the wedding on the front of the wardrobe. The calf-length green chiffon, which had looked exotic in the shop, now seemed rather ordinary. She imagined walking into the church with her hand on Jack's arm; the other guests would assume they were a couple. Her stomach fluttered with a confusing mix of emotions at the thought of it, and she quickly hung the dress away.

Melanie opened the window and stared at the view over the sea, wondering if Jack was doing the same thing. She'd told him she needed an hour alone before dinner to recharge her batteries, but now she realised she didn't want to wait here alone. If she knew Jack's room number, she could have walked upstairs to find his room, but she purposely hadn't asked.

Melanie took a tissue from her bag and her fingers brushed an envelope. With a rush of relief, she pulled it out. When she had left Ryan with her grandma, he'd given her the envelope with strict instructions that she mustn't open it until she arrived in Italy. This should pull her out of her melancholy mood.

Smiling, she ripped open the envelope and unfolded the piece of paper inside to reveal a drawing. Three people stood in a line holding hands: one tall with yellow hair, one middle-sized with long dark hair and between them a small one with short dark hair. Underneath them her son had written, *Jack, me and Mummy*, and in big sparkly rainbow-coloured letters, *MY FAMILY*.

* * *

The following afternoon as Jack drove to the wedding reception, Melanie avoided looking at him. With Ryan's picture of his 'family' still fresh in her mind, the romantic wedding ceremony in the small Italian church had been a poignant experience. She kept imagining Ryan in one of the cute little navy velvet pageboy outfits and the happy smile he'd have on his face if it were Jack standing beside her in front of the priest.

Yet she couldn't help remembering that her parents and her husband had shown her that the romantic notion of happy families was just that — a romantic fantasy.

Jack smiled at her. 'You're very quiet. Didn't you enjoy the ceremony? I thought women loved all that soppy stuff.'

'I'm fine.' She managed a smile. 'Just a little tired from the travelling yesterday.' She leaned her head back and closed her eyes to add weight to her words.

Conflicting emotions warred inside her. Why not let her friendly relationship with Jack progress naturally to something deeper? It didn't have to lead to marriage and forever. She knew he would be happy to take things further. Sometimes she caught him watching her when he thought she wasn't looking.

Yet the thought of allowing him any closer filled her with dread. She kept discovering new sides to Jack. What if she uncovered a side she didn't like? She'd thought her husband was a good man when she married him, so her judgment was obviously faulty.

'You sure you're all right, Mel?' he asked as he manoeuvred the car down a steep, narrow road towards a white villa swathed in bougainvillea.

'I told you, I'm just a little tired.'

When he slanted her a worried glance, she knew her excuse was wearing thin.

'You've been saying that all day.' Jack swung the car into the car park behind the villa and skilfully slotted the Ferrari between a low wall and a BMW. He frowned as he cut the engine and leaned back. 'You said the same thing yesterday evening after dinner when I suggested a walk on the beach.' He touched his fingertips to her cheek. 'Is something wrong?'

A shiver of pleasure from his touch caught her by surprise. She tilted her head out of his reach and rubbed her forehead, hoping he hadn't noticed her reaction. Keeping her feelings for Jack in check was proving far more difficult in Italy than it was at home. Work, Ryan and her strict routine kept her disciplined at home. Here all the boundaries were gone. It would be so easy to simply fall into his arms.

She forced a smile. 'I think I'm just a little overwhelmed. I haven't been away anywhere since before Ryan was born and then . . . ' She clamped her teeth over her lip. The more time she spent with Jack, the harder it became to keep her past a secret from him.

'And then what?'

'And then we never went anywhere very exciting. My husband didn't like to travel.'

'Why not?'

Melanie glanced up at the villa wide-eyed and pretended to notice it for the first time.

'Wow! What a fantastic place.' The building was perched on a rocky outcrop overlooking the sea. Sultry Italian music floated out of the open windows and the smell of spicy food scented the air. 'Pippa seems to have fallen on her feet.'

Jack angled his head in a way that said he knew she had deliberately changed the subject, but he didn't press her on it.

'No thanks to Pip. She's her own worst enemy. Apparently, she didn't tell Franco about the baby because she was frightened he wouldn't want the child. So she cut herself off from him and made herself miserable. If only she'd talked to him, all the heartache could have been avoided.'

He removed his sunglasses and aimed his far too perceptive blue gaze her way. 'Sometimes it's best to be

115

honest. Look at me. If I hadn't been honest how I felt about Stephanie, I'd be married to her now — and regretting it.'

'Would you?'

'Of course.' Jack captured her hand in his and squeezed. 'If I'd married Steph, I'd never have got to know you and Ryan.' He held her gaze for a long moment, her heart thumping as his thumb softly rubbed the back of her hand. Then he helped her from the car and motioned for her to precede him down the path into the villa.

The luxury building was full of beautiful people, their fluid, expressive Italian voices running descant to the music.

'There's Emily,' Jack said. Melanie stood on her toes to follow the direction of his gesture. She couldn't see Emily, but she noticed many women cast admiring glances in Jack's direction. In the sea of dark heads, his golden hair glowed like a beacon. Jack guided Melanie across the room, the pressure of his palm warm against the small of her back.

'Familiar faces, thank goodness!' Emily laughed as they approached. She sat alone at a small round metal table, legs crossed, a tall iced glass in her hand. 'The others have all abandoned me. Not that I'm complaining. Imelda is already tipsy; for the last half-hour she's regaled me with how wonderful Marco is.' She screwed up her nose. 'I spent the whole time biting my tongue so I didn't say what I think of him. Pip only has eyes for Franco, and my husband's holed up somewhere continuing his love affair with his mobile phone.'

Jack and Emily exchanged a brief kiss on the cheek, then he pulled out a chair for Melanie.

'Want a drink?' He scanned the room while she made herself comfortable. 'We can grab a glass of plonk from a passing waiter, or there's something fruity being served under the arch by the window.'

'Something non-alcoholic, if possible.'

'Heresy,' Emily hissed in good humour and then laughed. 'Go on. Live dangerously.'

The nightmare of Melanie's alcoholic husband seemed light years away, almost as if it had happened in a different lifetime. One glass of wine couldn't hurt, surely. 'Champagne then,' she announced, 'in honour of the occasion.'

Jack glanced at her, his hint of surprise morphing into a bone-melting smile. 'Don't move. I'll be right back.'

He lifted two crystal flutes filled with golden fizz from a tray bobbing past on a waiter's hand and took the seat beside her.

'To Pippa, Franco, the new baby and honesty,' he said, holding up his glass.

Honesty? Jack seemed obsessed with honesty today. Disquiet fluttered through her. As a matter of principle, she'd never lied to him about her identity. She'd even listed her husband's surgery as a past employer on her CV, otherwise she would have had to explain the huge gap in her employment history. Now the nightmare of the past felt like a ticking bomb that could destroy their friendship. She couldn't bear to see the heat in Jack's eyes replaced by the burn of condemnation.

Melanie touched her glass to his and he held her gaze as he sipped. 'They're dancing out on the terrace overlooking the sea. Want to take a spin around the floor with me?' Jack angled his head, a questioning look in his eyes, his lips curled in a self-deprecating smile as if he expected her to turn him down. A potent mix of longing and guilt seared through her, hot and fast.

'Don't worry about leaving me. You go and enjoy yourselves.' Emily squeezed Melanie's arm.

Melanie nodded and put her hand in Jack's. A dance was just a dance, not a life-long commitment. No big deal. Keep it casual.

She smiled and attempted nonchalance as Jack led her out to the terrace.

She knew her attempt had failed as he slid his arm around her waist and she tensed.

He leaned in and put his lips close to her ear. 'Relax, Mel.'

He drew her closer and the front of his jacket brushed her dress. 'It's been a long time . . . ' she blurted then flushed when she realised how that sounded. 'Since I danced, that is . . . like this . . . with a man . . . ' *Heavens, stop talking woman before you make a complete idiot out of yourself.*

'Don't worry.' He grinned down at her. 'I'll be gentle.'

As they twirled to the lilting notes of the Italian guitar, the tension in her neck and shoulders eased. The heady fragrance of bougainvillea and warm sea air lulled her, until she almost believed she was dreaming. Jack's hand on her waist guided her, his warm fingertips a gentle pressure on her skin through the chiffon. When the music slowed, he eased her closer and folded her into his embrace. She rested her cheek against his shoulder and closed her eyes.

She lost track of how long they danced for, but when she raised her head from his shoulder, the streaks of gold along the horizon had faded to a velvety blue and a small string of lanterns around the wall lit the terrace.

'You've been dozing on my shoulder,' he whispered close to her ear. 'Great for a chap's ego, that is.'

All the tension in her muscles had drained away and she did feel completely relaxed. 'Told you I was tired.' She smiled up at him and realised they'd stopped moving and were standing still as the sea of dancers circled around them.

'Come down to the beach with me,' he said.

Before she could consider her answer, Jack took her hand, led her to a break in the wall and down a flight of steps carved into the rocks. The tide had gone out since they'd arrived and the lantern-light glinted off ridges on the wet sand below.

Melanie stooped, pulled off her sandals and left them on a rock by the steps. The wet sand chilled her feet and a light breeze carried the tang of cooler air off the water.

'Are you trying to wake me up?' she asked.

'Definitely not.' Jack slipped his arm around her waist as they strolled. 'I like you sleepy and confused. You do what I say without arguing.'

'I don't argue.'

'What are you doing now?'

Melanie laughed, intoxicated with the pleasure of his company. Jack stopped and leaned back against a wall of rock, easing her around to face him. The sea sighed against the sand as gentle waves rolled in and out behind her. A breeze lifted her hair and he tucked loose strands of hair behind her ears and cupped the back of her head. 'You have beautiful hair. Do you know that?'

In the soft glow radiating from the villa, she stared at his lips. Would they be firm or soft? Against all common sense, she wanted to find out. She lifted her gaze to his. Twinkles of reflected lantern light glittered in his eyes. The moment seemed to stretch to eternity. His fingers flexed against her hair, pulled her closer. On a long, lingering breath, he breathed her name then lowered his mouth to hers.

Their lips touched, no more than a whisper of sensation. He drew back a fraction as if giving her time to change her mind. She curled her fingers beneath his lapels and kept her face tilted towards his. His lips were curved in a smile when he kissed her again. Melanie closed her eyes and lost herself in the flutters of pleasure coursing through her.

The sound of voices dragged her back to reality. Startled, she pulled away from Jack and a flicker of movement to the right caught her eye. A short distance away, in a nook in the rocks, Marco and a woman wearing a waitress's uniform were wrapped around each other.

The wonderful dreamy atmosphere evaporated. She and Jack had been kissing on the beach a few feet from Marco's sordid dalliance, and the pleasure she'd felt in Jack's arms now seemed tainted as she swallowed back a feeling of nausea. She'd allowed herself to be swept away by the romance of the place, just as she'd feared. Here she was, doing exactly what she'd promised herself she wouldn't do.

'What is it?'

Suddenly alert, Jack followed the direction of her gaze and then swore under his breath. 'I hope Mother doesn't know what he's up to. Last time this happened she wouldn't leave her bedroom for a week.'

Melanie found it hard to imagine Jack's capable, assertive mother hiding in her room, heartbroken over a gigolo half her age. But she shouldn't be amazed — she'd thought of herself as strong, but she'd allowed herself to be manipulated and deceived by her own husband.

Jack took her hand and led her back to the villa. She retrieved her sandals from the place she'd left them and they climbed the steps to the terrace. Once they reached the lit area, Jack paused and scanned her face, lines of tension bracketing the tight set of his mouth. 'Sorry. Very bad timing. I must find my mother and make sure she's all right.'

A search of the room where they'd left Emily drew a blank. When they looked outside, they found Emily, arms folded, sitting on the bonnet of a BMW with a resigned expression on her face. A balding man with sweat stains on his shirt sat in the car tapping on a laptop. She rolled her eyes as they approached.

'Apparently he absolutely must catch the last few minutes of trading on the New York stock exchange or the world will cease to exist as we know it,' she said.

'Have you seen Imelda?' Jack asked.

Emily's eyes narrowed. 'Not recently. Is there a problem?'

'Marco's doing his usual . . . '

'Not again. I swear that man is like a heat-seeking missile where pretty women are concerned.'

Jack sighed wearily. 'Well until Mum gives him the boot we just have to put up with him.'

'Come on, then,' Emily said, 'let's find Imelda before she catches Marco out.'

They split up and searched the building. Jack and Emily headed off to check the crowded areas. Melanie walked in the opposite direction around the deserted half of the terrace, away from the lights and music. When everything had gone wrong in her life, she had wanted to get away from people. If Imelda were upset, Melanie thought it more likely she'd be somewhere quiet.

When she came upon a flight of external stairs leading up to the roof terrace, she climbed them and let herself in through an ornamental gate draped with vines.

A few people were coming out of a

glass-walled lookout room artfully constructed along the seaward-facing side of the villa. Melanie stood in the open doorway and let her eyes adjust to the dim light. She could see a woman's legs stretched out from a large wicker chair, with three empty glasses on the table beside her. A chill of premonition passed through her. Even before she walked forward and saw the woman's face, she knew it would be Imelda.

Jack's mother sat slumped in the seat, appearing to be asleep. Melanie pulled over another chair and sat quietly beside her. Maybe she'd just had too much to drink and come up here to sleep it off. Should she wake Imelda and check she was okay? Melanie glanced out at the panoramic view while she considered. With a start that shook her to the core, she realised the view from the lookout included the beach where she and Jack had been so recently. If Imelda had been here half an hour ago, she'd have had a bird's eye view of Marco up to his tricks.

'Imelda,' she said softly. The woman didn't stir. Melanie shook her arm and still got no response. As she stood to go and find Jack, he appeared in the doorway.

'No luck downstairs,' he said. 'Have you found her?'

Melanie bit her lip and nodded. 'She's here.'

As Jack rushed forward, she added, 'Jack, look at the view.'

He glanced out the window over the beach where they'd seen Marco with the waitress and groaned.

'Mum.' Jack pulled a footstool in front of his mother and sat on it, clasping her hands. Then he frowned, pulled something from her fingers and held it up to the light. 'These are her sleeping tablets . . . '

Fear slashed through Melanie. She wasn't a doctor but working in a medical practice for seven years had taught her a lot about medicine. And there was one thing she knew for sure; sleeping tablets and alcohol did not mix.

'Let me see.' She pulled the pack from his hand and took it closer to the light. 'This is strong stuff, Jack. Even if she's only taken a normal dose, combined with the amount of alcohol she's drunk this evening it could be dangerous. We need to get her to a hospital immediately.'

Jack looked bemused for a moment then shook his head. 'Why would Mum be taking sleeping tablets now?'

'Perhaps she thought they were painkillers. It can be very easy to get confused when you've been drinking.' She reached out and laid a hand on Jack's arm, keeping her gaze steady on his face. 'I'm not sure, Jack. I'm just being cautious,' she said gently. 'I recognise the capsules because I've taken them myself in the past and I know how strong they are.'

'You've taken them?' A question hung in the air between them that would require her to bare her soul in answer and now was most certainly not the time for that.

Just at that moment, Emily ran into the room, her husband close behind her. 'Someone said there's a sick woman here — ' She stumbled to a halt and put her hand over her mouth when she saw Melanie and Jack.

'Call an ambulance, Em. Mum might have accidentally mixed alcohol and sleeping tablets.'

Emily snatched the mobile phone from her husband. 'For once I'm grateful you have this thing glued to your hand.'

After she placed the call, things happened fast.

Jack carried Imelda downstairs. When the ambulance arrived, they strapped her to a trolley and Jack climbed into the ambulance with her tossing his car keys to Melanie.

'I'll wait for you at the hospital in Naples. Collect my things from the hotel and meet me there.' The last thing she heard was Jack's muffled. 'Please.' Then the vehicle sped away, the flashing lights visible in the distance on the coast road long after the sound of the engine had faded.

Melanie clutched them to her chest and Emily put an arm around her shoulders. 'Don't worry, we can arrange for someone to pick it up. We'll take you back to the hotel to collect your things and then we'll go to the hospital together.'

Melanie was relieved. She couldn't have driven the Ferrari back to Naples, even if she were insured to drive it. Now Imelda was safely in the ambulance, Melanie's legs were shaking so badly, she could hardly walk, let alone drive.

* * *

Emily and her husband Doug dropped Melanie outside her hotel and arranged to collect her in an hour. Feeling shell-shocked, she went to her room and packed her things in a daze. Clasping the key to Jack's room like a talisman, she then rode the lift up to the next floor.

His room was a little further down the hall from the lift than hers. She unlocked the door, dropped her bag on the floor and glanced around, feeling as though she'd entered a forbidden sanctuary. The room was virtually the same as hers, except that it smelled of Jack. A tender feeling unfurled inside her, leaving her chest tight and her breath barely there.

What must he be feeling now? She didn't want to care this much, didn't want to hurt for him as if their feelings were so entwined she couldn't separate his pain from her own.

They were only friends, nothing more. Yet her memory kept replaying the agonised look on his face when he first saw Imelda slumped in the chair. That flash of vulnerability she'd seen in his eyes made Melanie's heart ache to comfort him.

She took a deep breath and straightened her shoulders before searching for his bag. Like her, Jack had only unpacked the clothes that needed to be hung up. She took a mental step back and adopted the detached mode she used when she handled guests' forgotten private possessions during her hotel work. With the quick efficiency born of long experience, she removed two shirts from hangers, buttoned, folded and packed them, then zipped the linen suit he'd worn on the flight yesterday into the suit carrier.

In the bathroom, she scooped up his toiletries from the tiled surface beside the basin and arranged them in the small waterproof bag. In the hotels where she'd worked, people often left sleepwear behind in the bed, so she checked under the bedcovers for pyjamas. She patted the covers and a piece of paper crinkled beneath the bedspread. Something Jack had been reading in bed must have become caught between the layers when the maid serviced the room.

She pulled out the paper from under the fabric and for a second, confusion held her immobile.

This was the picture Ryan had drawn for her, wasn't it? How had it found its way into Jack's bed? Then she noticed slight differences. The three figures were similar to those in her picture, except the man had a football at his feet. Underneath the characters, Ryan had written *Jack, me and Mummy* as he had on her picture, but he'd also signed his name on Jack's picture and the words *MY FAMILY* were written in neon colours.

Melanie stared at the picture, her thoughts a muddle of conflicting emotions. She was pleased Ryan felt close enough to Jack to give him the same picture he'd given to her. At the same time, a shadow of uneasiness fell over her. Despite her attempt to keep Jack as a friend and avoid any romantic entanglement, Ryan clearly saw them as a family unit.

Now she really must tell Jack about her past. Already she had let small details slip here and there, and she knew he was curious. The longer she let this situation continue, the more hurt Ryan would be if, once Jack found out, he didn't trust her any more and sacked her. She'd have to pray Jack would see things from her point of view.

6

Melanie thought she was too worried about Imelda to relax. In the event, as soon as she climbed in the back of Emily and Doug's car, she was out like a light. The journey passed quickly and only too soon the city lights and the bustle of Naples dragged her from her blissful stupor to face reality.

Doug quickly found the hospital and while he parked the car, the two women raced into the accident and emergency entrance. The waiting room was busy and they seemed to wait forever for a nurse to answer the receptionist's call to assist them.

A tall, austere woman in a nurse's uniform led them through a door into a quiet corridor and in halting English, asked what relationship they had to Imelda. After Emily explained, the woman beckoned her forward but put her hand up to Melanie and shook her head. 'No. You stay, *signorina*.'

'Must be family only.' Emily threw an apologetic glance over her shoulder as the nurse led her away. The double swing doors flapped shut behind Emily with a smack of finality, leaving Melanie standing alone.

Family only. Jack's family. Melanie didn't belong to Jack's family. Her chest felt hollow as she stared at the door, consciously breathing the horrid antiseptic smell in and out, fighting a sense of unreality, as though she'd become detached from her world and didn't belong anywhere.

She turned and wandered back towards the waiting room, her shoes squeaking on the rubberised floor. In contrast to the corridor, the waiting room was busy with a continuous procession of Italians coming and going. She stopped and looked round at the rows of plastic seats, not sure where to sit. A man holding a bloody towel to his head glared at her. Another man argued with the receptionist, his gravelly Italian harsh as he jerked his arms in angry gestures. A woman sat in a corner with a floppy child cuddled in a blanket, tears streaming silently down her face.

'Mi scusi!' The bark of a man's voice startled Melanie out of her contemplation. She hastily stepped aside to make way for an orderly pushing a patient on a trolley.

Melanie found a seat tucked away beside the wall and wrapped her arms around her ribs. She'd forgotten how much she hated hospitals. The smell and feel of the place dredged up memories she'd buried. Five years ago, she'd spent every waking hour for weeks inside one hospital or another while Ryan recovered from the accident and then underwent surgery on his arm and shoulder.

Just when the news of her husband's crimes hit the newspapers, she was stuck in the worst place possible. She would never forget the accusing looks the medical staff gave her, as if she had betrayed their profession along with her husband. But to a certain extent they were right. She should have known what he was up to. After all, she was his wife and as her mother always said, it was up to the woman of the house to watch the pennies.

The man arguing with the receptionist turned and started shouting at a nurse. Melanie rubbed her temples against the first sign of a headache. Maybe she should go outside and search for Emily's husband, but Jack had told her to meet him here. If she left, he wouldn't know where to find her. Although he must be so worried about his mother, she was sure he'd probably forgotten about Melanie. Maybe she should find a hotel for the night and come back tomorrow.

'Melanie! Where are you?' The alarm in Jack's voice cut through the hum of the waiting room. For a few seconds, all conversation ceased while people stopped what they were doing and looked around. She stood and saw him just inside the door, scanning the room.

'Here, Jack.'

His gaze flew to her and he strode over, pulled her into a hug that crushed the breath from her body and kissed the top of her head. 'Are you all right, Melanie? Emily shouldn't have left you on your own.'

'I'm fine. I can survive a few minutes alone.'

'You don't sound fine.'

'I'm just a little disorientated. It's been a long day.'

He stroked her hair and studied her face. 'Come on. Let's go back and see Mum.'

'They wouldn't let me in because I'm not family.'

Jack grunted in annoyance as he grasped her hand and pushed through the doors the nurse had closed in her face.

'They won't stop you this time. You're with me now.'

After negotiating stairs and corridors,

they reached the room. Jack released her hand and glanced through the glass panel in the door before opening it. Emily sat at Imelda's bedside, holding her hand, even though the older woman was asleep.

'Melanie.' Emily smiled apologetically. 'I didn't know what to do when they wouldn't let you through, so I came with the nurse and told Jack where to find you.' She wrinkled her nose. 'He wasn't happy they stopped you.'

'I wasn't happy you abandoned her,' Jack replied, closing the door quietly behind them. 'You could have been a little more creative, Em; told them she was my fiancée or something.'

'I'm fine.' Melanie tried to make light of the situation, but in truth, the hospital had really started to get to her before Jack appeared. 'More importantly, how is Imelda doing?'

'She woke up just before the ambulance arrived here,' Jack said, grimacing. 'You were right. She was trying to take some painkillers for her headache. Luckily, she recognised she had the wrong tablets and didn't take any. She was furious we had made such a fuss and embarrassed her. You should have heard the commotion she made when the doctor insisted she stay here overnight for observation, poor man!'

Melanie was reassured by the return of Jack's exasperated tone when he spoke about his mother, indicating he was less worried about her. She rubbed his arm, almost wishing she really were his fiancée so she could put her arms around him and give him comfort.

'The doctor reckoned she'll be fine to catch our scheduled flight home tomorrow afternoon,' he said. 'We can't do any more here tonight. Let's find a hotel for the rest of the night and come back in the morning.'

Emily and Melanie went to the door and paused as Jack dropped a kiss on his mother's forehead before he followed. When they reached the waiting room, Emily's husband Doug was asleep on a plastic chair between a woman holding a crying baby and a grumbling man with his arm in a sling. When Emily touched his hand, he opened his eyes, stood and nodded to Jack. Without saying a word, he led them back to the car.

Before they climbed in the car, Jack looked around the streets near the hospital. 'Let's try over there.' He pointed at a narrow old building with a blue neon sign over the door announcing it was a hotel. 'That's ideal. We don't want to waste time in the morning.'

They took their bags from the boot, and left the car parked where it was. Jack insisted on carrying Melanie's bag as well as his own, so she folded his suit carrier over her arm.

A string of small, blinking lights surrounded a tatty arched door badly in need of a new coat of paint. When they stepped over the threshold, the noise of the road outside the hospital died away, but a stale smell pervaded the air as

Melanie stared around the ancient reception area.

The reception desk was a dark nook in the wall, an old-fashioned table lamp with a green glass shade providing the only illumination. No doubt the muted lighting hid the worst signs of wear. She just hoped the place was clean.

The stress of the day suddenly caught up with her and Melanie flopped into a musty velvet chair beside a telephone kiosk. Emily took the matching armchair beneath the window opposite while the two men approached the reception desk.

Jack put down the bags and looked around. 'Buongiorno!' He repeated his greeting three times before an elderly man hobbled out from the shadows of a corridor. His English was very limited, but Jack managed to book rooms.

He passed a key over to Doug who then took Emily's arm to help her up from the chair. They said goodnight and headed for their room a short distance away on the ground floor.

'We're upstairs,' Jack said. 'Let's take the lift. I'm too shattered to face stairs.' Jack pushed the lift-call button and they stood side by side, staring up at the illuminated arc of numbers above the door as they ticked down while the ancient lift rattled and groaned.

A strange tension hummed between them, prickling Melanie's skin. She cast Jack a sideways glance, looking for a reason. 'Anything wrong?'

Jack rubbed the back of his neck then picked up the bags as the lift bell dinged. 'Sorry, Mel, you're not going to like this.' He looked at her, his face half in shadow, his eyes unusually dark. 'They only had two rooms available. We'll have to share.'

Her heart thumped as though she'd run up the stairs rather than taken the lift, as he stood just inside the doorway of their hotel room and watched Jack put their bags side by side on the end of the bed. Side by side! Her heart did a skip and a jump and couldn't decide if it wanted to race or stop altogether.

The bed looked small. It was a double, but an old-fashioned double. The trend for king-size beds obviously hadn't reached this part of Naples.

Jack unzipped his case and pulled out the toiletries bag she'd packed for him a few hours earlier in Positano. Because she'd already handled his personal possessions, the moment didn't feel as awkward as she had expected. Packing for him had helped her overcome the strangeness of being in his room.

He removed a piece of paper from his bag, unfolded it and held it up, grinning. 'I see you found the master-piece your son gave me.'

'Actually . . . ' Melanie unfastened her bag and pulled out her own picture. She unfolded it and held it up. 'Snap!'

Jack's grin turned into a laugh. 'Something tells me that little monkey of yours is matchmaking.' As the words left his mouth, Melanie involuntarily glanced at the bed. So did Jack. He gave her a wry smile. 'He'd be pleased with this set-up.'

Melanie smiled thinking about her son; he'd be so excited for them all to be together.

'If he were here, he'd probably be bouncing on the bed,' she said and the slight tension in her body melted away. This situation wasn't Jack's fault. She was certain he wouldn't take advantage of her. They just had to survive tonight and get Imelda home tomorrow, then they could return to normal.

If only she could forget that kiss on the beach.

'I'll sleep in the chair if you like.' Jack glanced round the room and his gaze settled on an armchair with an ornate gold frame that appeared to be designed for looks not comfort.

Melanie clenched and released her fingers a few times. She couldn't expect Jack to sleep on that impractical chair after the horrendous day he'd had.

'No. Don't be silly.' She opened the wardrobe door and to her relief found spare blankets and pillows. 'I'll make myself up a bed on the floor.'

'No way. I won't have you make do with the floor while I'm in the bed.' He wrested the blankets from her hands and spread them out on the threadbare carpet between the side of the bed and the wall. 'This will do for me. I'm so weary I could sleep standing up propped against the wall!' Jack laughed, but it sounded a little forced.

She busied herself with the things she needed from her bag to avoid looking at him. With her nightdress and toiletries bag bundled under her arm, she headed for the bathroom. 'All right if I go first?' she asked in her most efficient voice.

'Be my guest,' he said with a brief smile.

She quickly changed and cleaned her teeth, too tired to bother to remove the trace of make-up left on her face.

Jack averted his eyes as she hurried across to the bed and slid under the covers. 'Turn off the light,' he said. 'I'll find my way to bed in the dark.'

Melanie waited for Jack to enter the bathroom and close the door behind him before she clicked off the light-switch. She lay on her back and stared at the ceiling, willing the aching weariness to pull her into sleep. Perversely, she suddenly felt more awake than she had all day.

At first, the darkness seemed absolute, but as her eyes adjusted, she could see quite well by the thin slivers of light leaking into the room through gaps in the wooden shutters.

She turned on her side facing away from his makeshift bed and closed her eyes, but her eyelids didn't want to stay down. She fought the urge to let her eyes open and concentrated on breathing evenly. It would only take her a few minutes to fall asleep. By the time Jack finished in the bathroom, she'd be out for the count. If she weren't then she'd pretend.

The bathroom door creaked open and the bedroom was momentarily illuminated before he killed the bathroom light. All was silent for a second before she heard him padding across the floor. Once he settled, silence filled the room. Melanie concentrated on keeping her breathing shallow and even. If she breathed as if she were asleep, maybe it would induce sleep.

She'd never felt more awake in her life; every nerve in her body tingled and the image of him lying a few feet away wouldn't leave her head. Maybe if she distracted herself with more mundane thoughts, she could forget he was there. She thought about collecting Ryan from her grandmother's and what she needed to do when they returned to the hotel. That worked for a few minutes before her traitorous brain snapped back to images of the man on the floor.

She backtracked over the events of the day and remembered she had forgotten to tell Jack that the Ferrari was still at the villa. What a shame they wouldn't get to ride back along the beautiful coast road in the sports car. Marco had certainly spoiled their lovely weekend.

Marco! Had anyone told Marco what

happened to Imelda? Had anyone even told him they were all leaving? He'd flown over with Imelda and was due to fly back with her. He might be a rat, but he must have heard the ambulance siren and have worried when they all disappeared.

She rolled over to the far side of the bed and peered down at Jack. In the dim light, she could see his eyes were closed but his breathing sounded uneven. 'Jack,' she whispered. He opened his eyes and looked at her. 'We forgot to tell Marco what happened to Imelda.'

Jack made a noise of disgust and threw a forearm over his face. 'You disturbed me to talk about Marco?'

'He'll be worried about your mother.'

'I don't care, let him worry. This isn't the first time he's done this to her. I noticed that waitress he picked up, too; she looked like a supermodel.'

Something suspiciously like jealousy burned through Melanie. 'Does it really matter what she looked like?' After the words were out, she regretted the bite to her voice, but it was too late to take it back.

He lifted his arm and squinted at her in the dark. 'Only in as much as it makes my mother feel even more insecure. She worries enough as it is about getting old and losing her looks.'

Melanie hung over the edge of the bed and poked his arm determined to make her point. 'We'll have to tell Marco. Even if he is a rat he'll still be worried.'

'Oh, Mel.' Jack scrubbed a hand over his face. 'You're not going to make this easy for me, are you?'

'What?'

'Sharing the bedroom, of course.'

'Oh.' For a moment, she'd forgotten where they were. She was so used to spending time with Jack that being alone at night with him did not feel as strange as it should. She slid back and pulled the sheet up to her shoulders. 'Sorry.'

'This has been a difficult day. Every

time I close my eyes, I see my mother in that hospital bed. She's okay this time, but what will happen next time Marco upsets her?'

Melanie longed to touch him, comfort him, but she gripped her pillow instead.

'You remind me of her, you know,' Jack said, then added quickly, 'In a good way. I was all she had, like Ryan is all you have. She did so much for me. If it hadn't been for her encouragement, I wouldn't have followed my dream and tried out for the football team. My friends had mothers who pushed them towards law or medicine or something equally worthy. Yet Imelda listened to me. She let me do what was important to me. At the time I didn't appreciate her.'

Melanie thought of how her own mother had turned her back on her when she needed her most, and was grateful that Jack's mother had been there for him when his life had gone wrong. 'She's a strong woman, Jack.

I'm sure she'll get over this Marco thing soon and move on.'

Her hand instinctively went out to give comfort, just as it would with Ryan. When her fingers landed on his bare shoulder, she felt as though she was caught in a dream. In this unfamiliar bed in a nameless hotel, it would be so easy to give in to her desire, but in the cold light of day, she'd have to deal with the consequences. 'Jack . . . ' She bit her lip.

With a tortured sigh, he rose awkwardly from the floor and pulled on his shirt over the trousers he had not taken off. 'I'm going out for a while. You try to get some sleep.'

* * *

Jack sat on a stone bollard outside the hotel and welcomed the chill breeze blowing down from the foothills of Mount Vesuvius. What a stupid idea it had been for them to share the room. When he discovered the hotel only had two rooms, he should have volunteered to sleep in the car.

He closed his eyes, feeling drugged with exhaustion after the day's events. Immediately his mind conjured an image of Melanie as he'd left her alone in the bed, her chestnut hair spread across the pillow. He sighed and dragged his hand across his face.

Removing himself from temptation had been the right decision. If he'd given in to it, he knew exactly what would have happened in the morning. She'd have looked him in the face just long enough to tell him she'd made a mistake. The trust between them would have been gone and their friendship ruined.

Why wouldn't she let him get close to her? She had an invisible wall as tough as reinforced concrete protecting her heart. If only she'd confide in him, maybe they could work through what troubled her. But every little detail he learned about her past was hard-won.

Jack shivered in the breeze as he

looked up at the hospital windows reflecting the dull glow of light pollution from the city. Somewhere behind one of those windows, his mother slept.

He'd told Melanie that she was like his mother and it was true, in more ways than he'd admitted. Both women had been hurt by their husbands, but where Imelda dealt with the hurt by dating a string of unsuitable men, never allowing herself the chance of finding another stable relationship, Melanie chose the opposite tactic. She'd cut romance out of her life.

Over the past few months, he'd waited patiently for her to open up to him, with little success. The time had come for him to prompt her, to start asking questions. One way or another, he must uncover what troubled her and help her deal with it, or she would never move on.

When he had inadvertently blurted out to Stephanie that he loved Melanie, his subconscious must have known something that his brain hadn't caught on to yet — because he did love her; he wanted her in his life as more than a friend.

Now he had to persuade her that she wanted him, too.

*   *   *

When Melanie woke the next morning, she was alone in the hotel room. Jack's makeshift bed was gone, the blankets and pillow returned to the wardrobe. Did that mean he hadn't returned to bed — where had he slept? After the stress of his mother being rushed to hospital, he must have been exhausted, poor man. She shouldn't have worried about Marco last night when he really didn't deserve their concern. She should have let Jack sleep.

Once she got up, she realised all Jack's clothes were missing and his toiletries were not in the bathroom. She showered and packed quickly, trying to focus on the fact she'd be seeing Ryan later that day, rather than dwelling on what Jack thought of her.

When she was nearly ready to leave the room, a knock sounded on the door. She opened it to find Jack waiting outside, looking a little tired and crumpled, but still gorgeous enough to make her heart skip. Flustered, she fumbled the make-up bag in her hand and the contents scattered across the floor. She crouched to pick things up and, flipping her hair from her eyes, glanced up at him.

'You seem a little jittery,' he said, gathering up a lipstick and a couple of eye shadows that had landed in the hallway. 'Did you sleep all right?'

'Fine, fine.' Rather than look at Jack, Melanie gave the floor a once-over and zipped up her bag. 'What about you?'

'I managed.' He folded his arms and leant a hip against the doorway while she did a last check in the bathroom.

Nothing had happened between them, yet she was behaving like a guilty teenager. At last she halted her frantic activity, drew a calming breath and made herself look at him and ask, 'Where did you sleep?'

He walked to the window stared towards the hospital. 'On one of the chairs in the reception area downstairs.'

'Oh, Jack. You should have come back here.'

He shrugged. 'I can sleep on the plane. Anyway, we'll be home later. By the way, sounds like you were right about Marco.'

'In what way?'

'I rang Pip this morning. According to her Marco was beside himself when we all disappeared yesterday and took Imelda. Pip said he was in tears and he said the waitress came on to him.' Jack leaned a hand against the window frame and let his head hang. 'I think I'm losing my senses. I suggested Marco drive the Ferrari back to Naples and meet us at the airport today in time for the flight.'

'You have a soft heart.'

He laughed incredulously. 'More

likely I'm soft in the head. I hope it's the best thing for Mum.'

Melanie wandered across to join him at the window and stared at the gritty dirt gathered in the corners of the glass.

'Was it worry about your husband's drinking that drove you to use sleeping tablets?'

The soft enquiry came out of the blue and froze Melanie. Her fingers flexed against her side, curled into a fist.

When she didn't answer, he continued in a gentle voice. 'Remember you told me that your husband's accident was due to drunk driving.'

Melanie turned her back on Jack. 'I don't want to talk about this now. Wait until we get home.' She was too weary and stressed after the events of the last twenty-four hours to tackle a confession and Jack's reaction.

'Mel.' He laid a hand on her shoulder. She stepped away from his touch. She wanted to confide in him, tell him how she felt, but not now, not yet.

'Don't shut me out. Talk to me,' he whispered.

She imagined the look on his face when he discovered what her husband had done, what she'd stood by and let him do because she was too blind to see what the man she thought she knew and loved was capable of. In the village where they lived, people had whispered as she went past; how could his wife not have known?

Jack was close — too close — but she didn't want comfort, didn't deserve it. His arms started to circle her and she wasn't ready for this; she had so many worries crowding her mind that she couldn't handle a relationship. Especially when it might all end in tears again. She ducked out of his embrace and pushed past him to the door.

'Mel?' Jack extended his palms in supplication. 'Talk to me.'

'No, Jack. I'm not ready for this. I

warned you right at the start not to expect any romance.' She snatched up her bag from the bed, and dashed out of the room.

7

As soon as Jack's Mercedes stopped outside the bungalow in Brighton that evening, Melanie jumped out and ran up the narrow heather-trimmed path to her grandmother's front door.

The flight back from Naples had been a nightmare. Jack had spoken three sentences to her since they left the hotel by the hospital and she had replied to two of them with a nod and the third with a few mumbled words.

When the front door opened a few seconds after her knock, Melanie hugged her grandmother and closed her eyes, breathing in the reassuringly familiar scent of lavender. After hours of holding tight to her self-control, the comfort of the one person in the world she could trust nearly tipped her over into tears.

She finally forced herself to let go

and stand back. Her grandma took her hands and frowned. 'What is it, dear?'

'Nothing.' The older woman already had to field her parents' repeated demands to know where Melanie was and she didn't want to worry her any more. 'I'm just pleased to be back.'

As she walked into the tiny hall, the bathroom door burst open and her son came tearing out. 'Mummy, Mummy.'

'Oh my goodness. You're getting such a big boy.' She lifted him up and cuddled him. 'You'll be picking me up soon.'

Melanie breathed in the baby-shampoo scent of her son's hair before he wriggled to get down, saying, 'Where's Jack?'

A shaft of ice shot through Melanie. During the flight, she'd considered what to tell Ryan about their friendship with Jack, and she still wasn't sure what to say. She glanced over her shoulder, and saw Jack taking her bag from the boot of his car.

Ryan pushed past her and ran down the concrete path.

'Careful of the road, Ryan,' she shouted after him. She needn't have worried; he headed straight for Jack, making a noise like an aeroplane. Jack dipped athletically, swept Ryan up in his arms, spun him around and tipped him upside down. Her son screamed with delight.

'Ryan adores Jack, you know,' her grandmother said thoughtfully. 'He talked about him non-stop, 'Jack this and Jack that'. He seems like a nice man.' Her grandmother winked at her. 'Handsome as the devil as well.'

'Grandma, put a sock in it,' Melanie whispered and glanced at Jack, hoping he hadn't heard.

'Just because I'm old doesn't mean I haven't got eyes in my head. Maybe you've fallen on your feet this time.'

'Jack and I don't have that sort of relationship.'

Her grandmother gave her a disbelieving glance and Melanie turned away, too tired for explanations.

A terrible mix of sorrow and fear

twisted through her. Her relationship with Jack could never return to the easy friendship they'd shared before Italy.

Even though nothing physical had happened between them apart from that brief kiss, they'd crossed an invisible line. They couldn't go back, and she was dragging so much baggage from the past, she couldn't cope with any more emotional stress.

Once again, Ryan would be the one to suffer. Why ever had she allowed him to become so attached to Jack? She rubbed her temples, angry with herself. She'd foreseen this problem and still let it happen.

Holding Ryan's hand, Jack brought her son and her bag to the door. 'Both of these belong to you, I think.'

He greeted her grandmother with a charming smile and they exchanged a few pleasantries. Melanie and Jack were supposed to be staying at her grandmother's for the night and driving home the following day. The forced proximity would be embarrassing.

Jack obviously thought so as well, because he glanced at his car and ran a hand through his hair. 'Thank you for the invitation to stay, Mrs Marshall, but I think it's best if I find a hotel for the night and give you three some time to yourselves.'

'No! No!' Ryan hung on Jack's hand and tried to pull him inside. 'Mummy, tell Jack to stay. Tell him, tell him.'

Melanie's chest tightened until it was all she could do to keep breathing, let alone manage any words.

Her grandmother came to her rescue. 'Come on now young man.' She took Ryan's arm and made him look at her. 'Mr Summers has just flown back from Italy. He's tired and he won't get a good night's sleep on Great Nana's floor now, will he? You'll see him tomorrow when you drive home.'

Ryan's bottom lip jutted out, but he released Jack's hand and stomped into the bungalow.

'I'll collect you about nine tomorrow

morning, okay?' Jack asked with a breezy casualness.

She mimicked his attitude. 'That's fine, thank you. See you in the morning.'

With that, he strode away, climbed into his car and drove off without a backward glance.

Ryan hung on Melanie's leg and sulked. 'I wanted to play with Jack. Why didn't you make him stay, Mummy?'

Melanie's grandmother turned to face her and her fine grey eyebrows rose above the frame of her glasses. 'That's exactly what I'd like to know.'

She patted Ryan's head. 'You go and finish the picture you were drawing for Jack, pet. You can give it to him in the morning. Mummy and I need to have a talk . . .'

★   ★   ★

Jack fished out of his jacket pocket the velvet box containing the engagement ring he had planned to give Melanie and tossed it into his bag along with his hopeless dreams.

He stared morosely out over the Brighton seafront from his hotel window and sympathised with the rusty old freighter battling the waves.

The room service meal he'd ordered grew cold on the table behind him as he watched the passing traffic, a glass of whisky clutched in his hand. Despite the fact he hadn't eaten all day, the thought of food made him nauseous. Even the burning comfort of the alcohol had lost its appeal since he'd ordered it in a moment of desperation when he first arrived. He set down the glass, and in the space of five minutes unpacked, stripped off his clothes, washed and dropped into the bed.

Under the Mediterranean sun, he'd thought Melanie would let her guard down and he'd gently ease himself into her heart. The trip to Italy should have been a turning point in their relationship. He grimaced at the ceiling. It had been a turning point all right — a U-turn and everything possible had gone wrong.

He still couldn't fathom what he'd said to make her withdraw from him so completely. Whatever it was, he'd hit a nerve. How could he help her if she didn't tell him what was wrong?

The possibility he'd been trying to deny settled like a weight on his chest. Maybe she didn't want him and never would. He'd thought their friendship would develop into romance, that it was only a matter of time before she fell for him.

Jack threw a forearm over his eyes and tried to sleep. The aching void inside reminded him of the time, years ago, when his life had imploded, losing his football career and his fiancée within a week of each other.

He'd recovered from that; he would recover from this. Wouldn't he . . . ?

★ ★ ★

Melanie managed to avoid a cross-examination by her grandmother until after Ryan went to bed. As the two women finished drying up the dishes while the kettle boiled for coffee, her grandma pointed to one of the ladder-back chairs at the small pine table in the kitchen. 'Sit there, my girl. It's time for a heart-to-heart, and I don't want you getting too comfortable in an armchair and making the excuse that you're tired.'

They settled in the straight-backed chairs and sipped their coffee. 'Ryan thinks Jack is the bees' knees,' Grandma said, peering over the top of her reading spectacles.

'Yes, and don't I know it,' Melanie returned sourly.

'When you two dropped Ryan off, I'd have sworn the man was smitten with you. I truly expected you to return from Italy with a ring on your finger and a smile on your face; instead, you look like a wet weekend. What went wrong?'

Melanie pushed a weary hand through her hair. 'It's not that simple. Nothing went wrong as such. I'm just not ready to offer the sort of relationship Jack wants and deserves.'

'Why ever not?'

Melanie looked up with a frown. 'You know what Ryan and I have been through.'

'Yes, I do — and my question still stands. Why won't you give Jack a chance?'

Melanie drummed her fingers on the table. She didn't want this conversation now. She wanted to curl up in bed and forget today had ever happened. 'I'm not ready.'

'Darling.' Her grandma laid her hand over Melanie's. 'It's been five years, more than enough time to put what happened behind you and move on. Jack is not Marcus.'

Tears pricked Melanie's eyes. She concentrated on breathing until the need to cry subsided. 'How can I tell him what happened? Even mum and dad didn't believe my innocence. I couldn't bear it if Jack blamed me for not spotting what Marcus was doing the way everyone else does.'

'Not everyone.' Grandma tilted her head to the side and gave the encouraging little smile that made Melanie feel as though she was six again.

'Jack keeps interrogating me about my past. I just want him to stop asking questions and leave me alone.'

'Look at the situation from Jack's point of view. He obviously cares for you so he's trying to understand what's happened to make you so cautious about love,' her grandma said gently. 'No doubt, so he can find a way to help you overcome the problem. That's the way men's minds work. You give them a problem; they try to find a solution.'

Melanie pressed her fingers to her eyes. She remembered the protective way Jack had started to wrap his arms around her in the hotel, the strength of his warm body against her back, how patient he'd been before she ran out on him.

She dropped her head forward into her hands. 'I know I've been unfair to him. But I'm still not ready to take our relationship further. How can I get involved with a man when my personal life is such a mess?'

Quietly, her grandmother went into the hall then returned and placed a lined pad and pen on the table before Melanie. 'If you want to decide if Jack is a good sound man worth your time, do yourself a pros and cons list, darling. I always find it helps me make decisions. Write one list of all Jack's good points and another of his bad points. Then you'll be able to weigh them up and make a decision on whether he's a man you can trust to stand by you and Ryan no matter what life throws at you.'

Grateful for a way to clarify the muddled thoughts charging around her mind, Melanie dashed off her pros list: *Wonderful with children, especially*

Ryan; Ryan loves him; Ryan wants him for his daddy; patient; generous; fun to be with; good dancer; romantic; wealthy; good businessman; good looking; slightly strange but okay family; loves his mother; attracted to me.

She paused and looked up to discover her grandmother had left the room, so she added to her pros column, *gorgeous body and unbelievably sexy.*

Warming to her task, she started the cons list: *Jilted fiancée a few days before wedding.* Then she sat back and wondered if, irrational as it sounded, that should actually be in the pros column instead. He had only split with Stephanie because he thought it was the best thing for them both. Breaking off the relationship just before the wedding must have taken a lot of courage and, in a way, she admired him for it. She decided to leave the entry where it was for the moment and moved her pen down to the next line.

She bit her lip in concentration as she tried to think of more bad points. *His mother has a reptilian toy boy?* She couldn't put that down — Imelda's doubtful choice of boyfriend was hardly Jack's fault. *He never shuts down the office computer after he uses it?* That hardly qualified. He made her hot and bothered when he stood too close? He insisted on trying to dig into her past? He was too gorgeous for his own good?

Gradually the realisation hit her . . . she couldn't think of any faults worth listing.

The pen dropped from her fingers as a strange rush of heat raced from her toes to the top of her head. She put her hand to her throat, felt the initial flush of discovery fade as her old fear chilled her skin. What if Jack had given up on her, after her being hot one minute, cold the next?

Clutching the doorjamb to support her unsteady legs, she found her grandmother in the sitting room.

The older woman looked up from her magazine and pushed her reading glasses down her nose to peer over the top at Melanie. 'Any luck, dear?'

'Oh, Grandma, I think I've made a terrible mistake . . . '

★　★　★

The following morning Melanie was stationed at the living room window staring at the road and anxiously waiting for Jack. She had tried to contact him the previous night on his mobile phone but it must have been switched off. After a sleepless night spent tossing and turning, impatient for morning to arrive, she couldn't wait to apologise and find out if he was willing to give her another chance.

She was so keyed up that the sudden ring of the phone in the hall made her jump. When its insistent demand to be answered continued, Melanie relinquished her place by the window and hurried to the hall door.

'Grandma,' she shouted towards the bedrooms, 'phone for you.' But when her shout got no response, she stepped closer to the phone, a chill of foreboding passing through her. There was no answering machine to screen the call but she couldn't just ignore it in case it was something important.

Frustrated with herself for being so tentative she snatched up the handset and answered briskly.

'Melanie, is that you?' The sound of her mother's voice closed her throat with a crush of mixed emotions and for long moments she could barely breathe. She closed her eyes, fighting a mental battle over whether to slam the phone down.

'Answer me, Melanie. After all this time, the least you can do is speak to me on the phone.' Her mother's initial hesitancy had vanished by her second sentence to be replaced by the firm, slightly critical tone that snatched Melanie back to her youth.

'It's me, Mum,' she whispered feeling like a child again.

'I've been trying to contact you for three years, Melanie. Your father and I want to know where you are, to see our grandson.'

'You didn't want anything to do with us five years ago when you turned your back on me in the pub and ignored me in front of half the village.' Melanie had rehearsed this conversation in her head many times, but now it was happening, the anger she'd expected didn't come. She simply felt tired, bone weary from the stress, the uncertainty, the loneliness, the constant moving.

The static on the line buzzed in her ear. 'You can't blame us for being shocked by what happened,' her mother offered defensively. 'Everyone in the village thought you and Marcus had planned the swindle together. It was only when the police cleared you that we realised we'd been too quick to judge.'

And there lay the rotten heart of the problem. Melanie kneeled down beside the telephone table and cradled her head in her hand. 'I'm your daughter, for heaven's sake!' she almost hissed, tears pricking her eyes. 'You should have known me better than that.'

'I'm sorry, Melanie,' her mother said, finally sounding almost contrite. 'You must understand, Dad and I were under a lot of pressure at the time. We're not mind readers and you didn't confide in us. What did you expect — '

The rest of her mother's excuse was cut off as Melanie softly replaced the receiver. She stayed on her knees until the phone resumed its shrill ring. Then she stood and walked away.

'Why does that blasted phone keep ringing this early in the morning?' her grandmother grumbled, hurrying through from the bedroom. The moment she saw Melanie she stopped in her tracks. 'Your mum?'

At Melanie's nod, her grandmother hugged her and stroked her hair. 'Your mum and dad only want to try to mend fences, pet,' she said soothingly.

'I can't do that. I can't forgive them.'

She'd expected the family she loved to believe her innocence and support her without question — as she would support Ryan. And as Imelda had supported Jack.

How could they have thought she would swindle old folks out of their savings? They didn't know her at all — and they certainly didn't love her.

Melanie wiped her nose as the doorbell rang and Ryan ran to open the front door shouting, 'Jack, Jack, where have you been? I've been waiting for you forever!'

Standing aside, Melanie let Jack sweep her son into his arms and swing him around. Tears pricked her eyes anew as Jack hugged Ryan and her darling little boy hugged him back, his eyes tightly closed as if he were concentrating every scrap of his energy on the hug.

She wanted so much for them to be happy together, but she felt as though her heart had been squeezed until it was numb, her love and trust wiped out by the pain of the past.

Jack was a decent, honourable man; he deserved a woman who could love him, and she wasn't sure she could ever again love anyone but Ryan.

Jack watched Melanie lug Ryan's bag down the path like a zombie, her shoulders sagging, her normally sharp, intelligent gaze dim and weary. When he arrived, she had barely acknowledged him. She had an air of defeat about her that set alarm bells ringing in Jack. After he hefted her bag and Ryan's into his boot, he caught her arm as she turned towards the car door. 'Are you all right, Mel?'

Her only response was a nod before she pulled on her arm and he released her. He'd held out a last hope that she might have reconsidered her feelings overnight and be conciliatory this morning, but he'd hoped in vain.

As Jack drove back to Devon, Melanie brooded silently beside him while Ryan kept up an animated stream of chatter about football before falling asleep for the second half of the journey.

As they neared the end of the journey, she became jittery. Every few minutes she glanced over her shoulder to check Ryan in the back of the car. Jack could hardly bear to see her like this after the moments of happiness they had shared in Italy when she had laughed, relaxed and let him get closer — before everything went pear-shaped. If only she would unburden herself of whatever was troubling her and let him help.

He'd told himself he would give up on trying to win her heart, but he couldn't. He reached out a hand, caught hers and squeezed. 'Don't look so worried. Life's good. Be happy.'

She glanced over her shoulder at Ryan sleeping and released a long sigh. Then, fixing her gaze on the windscreen, she spoke in a flat toneless voice.

'There's something you deserve to know . . . my husband persuaded some of his elderly patients to give him their money to invest. He used it to pay off his own debts.'

It took Jack a moment for what she said to sink in before he realised the importance of her words. His breath hitched as he remembered the case, the newspaper headlines condemning Doctor Marshall and his wife for preying on trusting elderly patients. The son of one of the old ladies who lost money was an MP, so the case received heavy national coverage.

Before he could respond, Melanie continued.

'Everyone in Littlechurch thought I was guilty as well. They couldn't believe I lived and worked with Marcus but didn't know what he was up to.' She cast Jack a quick sideways glance, tears gleaming in her eyes. 'The truth is, we hardly spoke at home. After Ryan was born, Marcus withdrew from me and I didn't know what went on inside his head.' She sighed again and added, 'I'll understand if you want me to resign.'

'Of course I don't want you to resign.'

Jack wanted to stop the car and hold Melanie, comfort her, but she had chosen to tell him on a busy stretch of dual carriageway where it was impossible to pull over.

'I don't believe for a moment you were guilty of any wrongdoing. You were as much a victim of your husband's actions as the pensioners he robbed.'

She pressed her hand to her mouth and angled her head away so he couldn't see her face. He swore silently to himself when traffic slowed to a crawl as holidaymakers heading to the West Country overloaded the road and held him up, when all he wanted to do was find a turn-off and stop the car.

'Melanie,' while they were moving slowly he took a hand off the steering wheel to gently rub her shoulder.

'The trouble is, I am to blame,' she said. 'I should have noticed what Marcus was doing. I knew he was behaving strangely but I ignored it because I was so wrapped up in caring for Ryan.' She glanced across at him. 'I didn't want to know.'

'It's not your fault, Mel. And it

happened five years ago. Can't you put it behind you?'

'The past follows me like a shadow. I've been sacked twice in the last five years because employers discovered who I was and didn't trust me.'

Jack clenched his jaw at the injustice, then realised with a sick jolt that she had been worried about telling him for the same reason. 'You didn't really think I would sack you, did you?'

'Not once I got to know you.' After five minutes' silence while she gnawed on her lip, she asked, 'Are you planning to tell your family about my history?'

'It's none of their business.' They weren't going to marry her, he was — once he persuaded her to accept his proposal.

'What if they find out? Your mother might not want me working at the hotel.'

'Mother will be fine, don't worry.' Despite his reassurance, he wasn't sure how his mother would take the news.

'Sorry if you think I'm being paranoid. I'm not used to people being understanding.'

The façade she presented to the world was of a strong, efficient woman, but all the condemnation she'd suffered in the past had left deep wounds and it was obvious that Melanie believed she was guilty — not because she'd known what her husband was doing, but because she hadn't realised and stopped him.

However hard Jack tried to make her happy, he'd fail unless he could make her let go of the past.

* * *

As soon as they arrived home, Jack went to visit his mother to find out how she was. He also wanted to pre-empt any problems she might have with Melanie's background.

Imelda Summers was sitting in state in the sun lounge on a huge leather chair stacked with cushions, a light blanket over her legs and a tall glass of something he sincerely hoped was non-alcoholic on the table beside her.

'Jack, darling.' She received her obligatory kiss on the cheek then peered around him towards the door. 'Where's Melanie? I hope you haven't lost her already.'

'Not lost, just dealing with life — she has a son, remember.'

He noted her self-satisfied little smile with interest. She'd made no comment to him about Melanie's son, but the ready-made grandchild was obviously considered an asset.

'Have you set a date?' Imelda asked. Straight for the jugular. Even she was usually a little more diplomatic in her attempts to marry him off.

Although Jack had every intention of asking Melanie to marry him as soon as he thought she'd accept, he couldn't resist having a little fun. Jack dropped into one of the other armchairs, now denuded of cushions, and wriggled to get comfortable while he considered tactics. Unfortunately, feigning ignorance didn't usually work with Imelda as she knew him too well, but it was worth a try. 'A date for what?'

'Don't play games with me, young man.' His mother gave him a quelling look. 'You know exactly what I mean.'

'No, Mother. No date.'

'Then hurry up. I always think a summer wedding is preferable.' She wagged a finger at him. 'And you can't use the excuse that you aren't able to book a venue for the reception.'

'Actually, Melanie's done such a good job of promoting the hotel that it's fully booked over the summer. We'll have a job fitting in our own reception until the autumn.'

'I wasn't talking about the hotel.' His mother looked at him over her glasses, which she only used at home, never admitting the need for them in public. 'I meant here.'

Jack glanced around and frowned. 'You want hordes of people tramping through your home?'

189

'Hordes? It'll only be family and friends, Jack. You make them sound like a herd of wild animals. Tramping, indeed.'

Marco sauntered in with a bowl of chocolate ice cream topped with fluffy whipped cream and chocolate chips.

Jack's mother snatched off her glasses and hid them beneath the blanket. 'Oh, my darling. You do spoil me.'

Jack ground his teeth and resisted telling Marco to go and crawl down the nearest drain. Such a comment might make Jack feel better, but wasn't the way to get his mother on side.

'I was hoping to talk in private, Mum.' Jack certainly didn't want Marco in on Melanie's secret.

His mother looked up and pursed her lips. He watched the internal battle on her face before she turned to Marco and said, 'Would you get me a coffee, too, darling?'

Marco aimed a scowl at Jack then slouched away. Toy Boy would return in a few minutes, which didn't give Jack long, so he'd have to get straight to the point. 'I plan to ask Melanie to marry me as soon as the moment's right,' he blurted out.

His mother beamed at him. He smiled with her, hoping he wasn't giving her false hope. Despite external appearances, she was very much like Melanie. She blamed herself for her husband leaving just as Melanie blamed herself for her husband's crimes. He hoped his mother would see the similarities, too, and empathise with her.

'Melanie told me something about her husband that you should know before I ask her to be my wife.'

As he related the story of Doctor Marshall, his mother listened in silence, her face tense, her jaw clenched. Jack left nothing he knew out, but he made sure he stressed how Melanie had tried to protect Ryan, and what she'd suffered since. When he finished, tears shone in his mother's eyes.

She took out a tissue and wiped her cheeks. 'I had no idea. That poor woman and her little boy. Well, at least she's found you.' She reached out a hand and squeezed his arm. 'You'll be good for her, Jack.'

Jack released a breath he didn't realise he'd been holding and smiled. 'I know. But first, I have to persuade her to marry me. I get the impression she's terrified the past will catch up with her, so we mustn't let anyone else know who she is. You remember how the press hounded me in the past? Well, they did the same to her.'

'I won't tell anyone. You can be sure of that.' As his mother finished speaking, Marco breezed back into the room and set a steaming coffee cup on the table beside Imelda.

He smirked at Jack with a glint of something unsettling in his eyes. 'If you have finished with your private talk, may I have my lady love back?'

Jack tried hard not to cringe. 'I'd best get back to the hotel.'

He bent and kissed his mother's cheek, then headed for the door. Before he left, he paused and looked over his shoulder. Marco had picked up Imelda's hand and pressed his lips to her fingers, but his gaze was still fixed on Jack.

8

After three weeks during which Melanie settled back into the routine of work and Jack returned to being a friend without any romantic pressure, she began to relax. The awful memories dredged up by speaking to her mother faded to the back of her mind again and she finally felt ready for a romantic dinner with Jack while Ryan stayed the night with Emily and her sons.

Jack had been so supportive when she admitted her past that she felt almost silly for making such a big thing out of it. Her mind returned often to the pros and cons list she had compiled, wondering if just maybe she and Jack could make each other happy after all. Melanie had begun to let her guard down and for the first time in five years, she was truly happy.

They had both taken Saturday

morning off from hotel duties to go for an idyllic walk in the countryside, followed by an early lunch at a pub. They had arrived home and were having a coffee in Jack's back garden when Ryan appeared through the gap in the hedge from Melanie's flat, closely followed by Emily.

'Found you!' she said with a laugh. 'Hope you made the most of the alone time. This little chap has had lunch. Can't stop, as my two are waiting in the car.' With a wave of her hand, she turned to go.

'Mummy, Jack!' Ryan dashed across the grass and started to scramble up on the bench between them. Jack gave Melanie's shoulder a squeeze as she slid aside to make room for her son. He kneeled between them, curled an arm around each of their necks and pulled them all together for a group hug. She laughed as her nose squashed against Jack's cheek and a warm glow of contentment settled inside her.

Ryan held them captive for a few

minutes then excitedly clambered to Jack's lap. 'When are you going to be my daddy?'

Melanie thought she was past blushing over things her son said to Jack, but heat rose up her neck and she knew her cheeks would be pink.

'You're the master of tact, young man,' Jack said tweaking Ryan's nose. 'But that's up to your mum.'

Jack looked at her and so did Ryan.

'I might be old-fashioned, but I thought it was still the man who did the asking,' she returned with an embarrassed laugh.

Jack set Ryan on the bench again, fished around in his jacket pocket and produced a small red velvet box.

Melanie's heart leaped at the sight of it. He couldn't be about to propose, surely?

Ryan started bouncing again, but Melanie put an arm around him to hold him still. 'Shoosh, sweetheart. You need to sit quietly for a few moments.'

Jack smiled, a touch self-consciously.

'I've been carrying this around for a long time, waiting for the right moment . . . '

He lifted the box lid and took out a solitaire diamond ring.

'Melanie, will you marry me?'

For several moments, words spun around in her mind but didn't make it to her mouth.

Ryan yelled, 'Yes, yes!', picked up her hand and held it out.

Jack kept his gaze on her face and the vulnerability in his blue eyes tore at her heart. 'Yes,' she whispered. 'I'd love to.'

Jack laughed, the sound as much relief as pleasure, and slid the ring onto her finger. Ryan lifted her hand and turned it back and forth in the sunlight. 'Look at it sparkling, Mummy.'

'We were right,' Jack said. 'Your son is definitely a matchmaker. He can make a career of it someday — he'd corner the market.' He leaned close and kissed her cheek. 'All your troubles are behind you, Mel. Only good things from now on.'

Jack wrapped his arms around both her and Ryan and smiled. 'I feel like I've waited a long time for you, but you're worth the wait, my darling.'

Melanie hadn't felt this light inside since the first time she held Ryan. She closed her eyes and revelled in the safety of his embrace. Finally, she and her darling boy could have a fresh start and a chance of happiness.

Jack put his arm around her shoulders and they wandered back to her flat to fetch some colouring books to keep Ryan occupied in the hotel office while she did a few hours' admin work. As Melanie pushed open her front door, it jammed on the local papers and a heap of letters.

'What on earth?' Melanie picked up a few of the envelopes, checking the addresses. She half expected to find they'd been wrongly delivered. Jack stooped and picked up one of the local newspapers. The lazy smile fell from his lips and tense lines appeared on his forehead. 'Jack. What is it?'

When he didn't answer, she tried to pull the newspaper from his hands.

'No.' He hung on, twisting it so she couldn't read the front, his eyes bleak.

'Jack! What is it? Let me see.'

After a few more seconds' resistance he breathed a curse and let go. She turned the paper over to read the headline, heart thumping so hard her ribs hurt.

Doctor Conman's Widow in Town.

* * *

Jack watched Melanie flop onto a kitchen chair as though her legs wouldn't hold her, the newspaper crumpled in her hand. A chill fist clenched in his gut.

'Mel.' He crouched beside her, tried to unclench her stiff fingers from around the paper. 'It'll be all right. It'll blow over.'

The blood drained from her face leaving her pale, her eyes huge and dark. Her gaze travelled to the scattered

199

heap of envelopes he'd put on the table. 'How did the journalist find out?' she whispered. 'You're the only person I've told.' Her gaze came back to him, no accusation in her eyes, just confusion and hurt.

'I didn't tell them, Mel. I promise.'

But he had told his mother. He hadn't thought of that as breaking Melanie's trust, because he'd wanted his mother's support and understanding, but he had gone behind Melanie's back to save her worrying. He couldn't believe his mother would have told the press. Maybe she'd let a detail slip to a friend, but surely that couldn't account for the newspaper headline.

'Then how?' Melanie looked so lost he wanted to comfort her, but when he put his arms around her she remained rigid, unyielding. She'd withdrawn and shut him out — just as she had a few weeks ago.

Ryan ran in crying, holding out his finger. 'I got a splinter, Mummy.' As if someone had thrown a switch inside her, Melanie's expression firmed. She stood and, moving like an automaton, went into action. She bent and hugged Ryan, kissing his hair. 'You'll have to be a brave boy while Mummy gets it out for you. Jack will give you a hug to make it better.'

Jack took a seat at the table, and held out his arms for Ryan while Melanie found a needle and efficiently removed the splinter. Brightly efficient, she returned the needle to its case and smiled at Ryan. 'I think you deserve a treat after that.'

Ryan wriggled out of Jack's arms and accepted a small box of raisins and a cup of juice. Melanie then pulled on rubber gloves and started wiping and tidying in earnest. Jack was almost more shaken by her stoic control than the newspaper headline. He'd expected her initial shock to be followed by tears and recriminations.

To someone who didn't know her, everything in the kitchen would appear normal, but being busy must be her

way of coping. When Jack had inter-
viewed her for the hotel job, he'd been
impressed by her brisk efficiency, her
focus. He hadn't realised then that she
was focusing on her work to block out
her pain.

'Mel.' He had to crack the brittle
shield of efficiency she used to keep the
world, and him, at bay before it was too
late.

She looked up, eyebrows raised. 'Sorry,
Jack. Do you want another drink?'

'No. I just — '

'Another coffee maybe,' she said in
her crisp, no-nonsense voice he'd heard
a hundred times while she was at work
in the hotel. Her 'keep your distance,
I'm busy' voice.

'Okay,' he agreed, bemused. He was
used to soothing his mother who always
made a performance of her emotional
traumas. Dealing with Imelda was like
talking a jumper down from a window
ledge. Melanie's emotional retreat was
something new to him. Words weren't
the answer, so he went up behind her,

gently clasped her upper arms and held her still.

'Mel,' he whispered against her ear. 'Stop this.'

He tried to turn her into his arms, but she shrugged away his hands, fetched a mug from the cupboard and poured his coffee.

'Life has to go on, Jack. I've been here before and it's the only way to cope.' She gave a meaningful look in Ryan's direction. 'I have someone else to consider, so for me, falling apart is not an option.'

With a hollow pulse of certainty, he realised she would do whatever she could to shelter Ryan from being hurt. Even if that meant packing up and moving on to a new place where they weren't known. He looked at the ring on her hand that he'd carried around in his pocket for a month or more, waiting for the right moment to lay his heart on the line. It was still on her finger, but mentally, she'd already taken it off.

Jack persuaded Melanie to take a hot

shower, hoping it would relax her. While Ryan coloured a picture on the kitchen table, Jack read the newspaper article, praying a sharp journalist had somehow discovered Melanie was in town and the timing of his chat with his mother was coincidental. When the article referred to an anonymous source, a shot of anger and betrayal went through him.

Ryan got bored with colouring and piled the letters into a neat heap. He gave a cheeky grin. 'I've made a letter castle.'

Jack forced himself to smile back. 'So you have.' It dawned on him how many letters there were. With a flash of dread, he realised some were probably from people who'd read the newspaper. He pulled out one from a bank and another from a sales catalogue, left them on the table and folded the rest into the newspaper. He really shouldn't open letters addressed to Melanie, but he planned to screen them and remove anything offensive before she read them.

As soon as he heard the bathroom door open he shouted, 'I'm going home for a short while.' A few minutes later, he unlocked his back door, dumped the bundle of paper on the table and went straight for the phone. He dialled his mother, and the housekeeper answered. Jack drummed his fingers on the table and stared at the newspaper headlines while he waited for his mother to come to the phone.

'Jack darling, to what do I owe this pleasure?'

'Did you talk to anyone about Melanie's past?'

Silence for a few seconds. 'No.'

'Have you seen the Courier?' he asked briskly.

'I haven't had time. It's here somewhere. All the newspapers normally get put on the hall stand.'

'Find it. Look at the front page.' Jack waited while his mother went to fetch the newspaper.

'Good heavens!' The shock in his mother's voice told him she wasn't the one who'd spilled the beans. Not that he'd thought she was, but the confirmation eased the tension in his neck as his mother asked, 'Poor Melanie. Is she all right?'

'What do you think?' Jack pinched the bridge of his nose, regretting his harsh tone. He had a nasty suspicion he knew who the informant was. 'Did you tell anyone? Anyone at all?'

'Well . . . ' He heard a slight catch in his mother's breath. 'Marco overheard some of our conversation. He asked me about Melanie. I couldn't refuse to tell him.'

'Of course you could!' Anger surged through Jack, burning in his blood, making his head feel as though it would explode. 'Marco's untrustworthy — you know that, Mum.'

At his mother's small sound of distress, a flicker of remorse made Jack wish he could be gentle, but anger drove him on. 'He's a leech, sucking you dry, spending your money. You give him everything he asks for, yet he sold

Melanie's story to the local rag and they couldn't possibly afford to pay more than a few pounds.'

'But Jack, just let me talk to — '

'Get rid of him, Mother. I proposed to Melanie this morning and she accepted. Half an hour later, she saw that headline. You know what she'll do now, don't you? She'll take her son and leave town. Her priority is keeping Ryan safe from this.'

Small sobs sounded on the other end of the line, but Jack couldn't stop. 'I'm going to lose her and Ryan, and it's Marco's fault. Get rid of him, or I'll never speak to you again.'

He slammed down the phone and stared at the wall, his breath coming in short, harsh gasps. He could blame Marco all he wanted, but if he hadn't gone behind Melanie's back to speak to his mother, Marco would never have found out.

If he lost Melanie, it would be his own fault.

Jack went back to Melanie's flat mid-afternoon, where he tried to coax her into discussing how she felt about the newspaper article, but so many emotions were churning inside her she couldn't get her thoughts straight. After a painful fifteen minutes over a cup of tea during which he probed gently and she shook her head a lot, Jack suggested he take Ryan to his house for the rest of the day to give her time to think.

She let them go because the effort of keeping up a cheerful front for Ryan was draining her. She was not fit company for anyone at the moment.

As soon as they left, Melanie pulled out her plastic box of cleaning supplies from underneath the sink and started to try to scrub and wash her frustrations away. When exhaustion finally caught up with her, she paused her frantic cleaning and closed her eyes. As if sensing she was weakening, the fears she'd kept locked away escaped her control and raced back into her mind.

How can I stay here now?

Tears she'd held inside for hours pricked the backs of her eyes. The news would soon be round the whole town and everyone would look at her as they used to in Littlechurch — as though she was a criminal. Thank goodness it was the school holidays so Ryan was spared the playground bullying.

Gritting her teeth, she scoured a dark scuff left on the grey kitchen tiles until her arm ached. She sat back on her heels and massaged the muscles in her forearm. She must do what was best for Ryan, but how could she take him away from Jack? Ryan already loved Jack like a father. And she loved him, too.

How can I leave Jack?

Pain gripped her chest so hard she struggled to suck in air.

How can I stay with Jack?

She couldn't bear the thought that he'd be subjected to the gossip and ridicule she'd have to put up with. She couldn't work at the hotel, either.

Guests might boycott the place if they knew she worked there, and if Jack married her . . .

Melanie swapped the scourer to her other hand and rubbed at another spot of dirt. It was always an upheaval to move on, but she'd never before had to leave behind someone she loved.

Her gaze rose to the diamond ring left safely on the windowsill while she cleaned. The stone concentrated the sun into a shimmering point of brilliance.

How could she put it back on her finger now?

She should never have become involved with Jack. Anyone associated with her would be a target if things turned nasty, as they had before. She was the bad apple in the barrel that turned all the others rotten.

Late in the afternoon, when Melanie had worked her way through most of the flat and was giving the bath a thorough clean, the phone rang. Ryan asked if he could stay over at Jack's house that night. Although her heart ached at the thought of being without him, she agreed immediately. In some of the other places they'd lived, horrible things had been posted through the letterbox and stones thrown at the windows. She wanted Ryan out of the house as much as possible.

At six p.m. while she was sorting through Ryan's toy cupboard and washing dirty plastic toys, someone knocked on the front door. With chills racing up and down her spine, she peered through the peephole. Jack and Ryan stood on the mat holding a package. Her initial burst of pleasure faded to concern as she opened the door. 'I thought he was staying with you tonight?' she fired at Jack before he could open his mouth.

'Look, Mummy, fish and chips.' Ryan raced past her towards the kitchen with the white plastic carrier bag in his arms.

Jack raised his eyebrows in response to her comment, then put his hand on her back, eased her inside and shut the door. 'It was Ryan's idea he should stay with me, but I don't think you should be alone tonight.'

Melanie busied herself laying out plates and cutlery on the table. 'Hands, Ryan,' she reminded him as he started to pull out his chair. She watched out of the corner of her eye as Jack pushed Ryan's footstool up to the sink. He and Ryan made a game out of washing their hands together with a great deal of laughing and splashing.

Her throat clogged and she bit her lip to stop tears falling. She opened the fridge door and crouched to find the tomato ketchup, using the time to gather her composure.

'I thought I might sleep here on the sofa tonight?' Jack said as she returned to the table. 'I don't want you two to be alone.' A moment of loaded silence. 'Unless you don't want me here, of course,' he added softly.

She wanted to be left alone so she could hold herself together and not have him prodding and poking at her psyche, working his way inside where she couldn't control her feelings.

'Thank you for offering, but we'll be all right,' she said without looking up at him. If she saw the concern in his eyes she might break.

She fiddled with her food, removed some batter from the cod and ate a few flakes of white fish. Ryan helped himself to a blob of tomato ketchup then dipped in a chip, using his fingers. 'Knife and fork please, Ryan,' she said automatically.

'You can't eat fish and chips with a knife and fork,' Jack said with forced humour. 'You have to use your fingers.' He ducked his head to see her face, then smiled as he picked up a chip and popped it into his mouth.

Ryan laughed and ate another chip, squashing the whole thing into his mouth with the flat of his palm. Somewhere inside, she knew Jack was only trying to lighten the mood, but a frisson of anger passed through her. One thing she could control was her son, and she wouldn't have Jack undermining her authority.

'If you put too much in your mouth you won't chew it properly and you'll get tummy ache.' She glared at Jack, although her words were for Ryan.

Ryan wrinkled his nose in a cheeky expression and stuffed another fat chip into his mouth.

'Ryan!' Her voice rose as panic spiralled through her.

Ryan stopped chewing, a look of wide-eyed confusion on his innocent little face.

Everything was falling apart. She'd been able to protect him when he was tiny, but now his life was more complicated. He would have to go back to school in September and face up to people who might pick on him because of what his father had done. How would he react? Would it leave him mentally scarred?

Jack's hand closed over hers on the table. The panic subsided, but the fear didn't fade. She couldn't stay here and let Ryan suffer.

When they finished dinner, Ryan said, 'I want to play with Jack. You wash up, Mummy.'

Jack crouched and held Ryan's shoulders. 'Mummy isn't just here to clear up after us, kiddo. She likes to have fun as well.'

Melanie waved her hand in acquiescence. 'You two play. I'll tidy up the kitchen.' She'd rather do that anyway. It kept her occupied so she didn't think. Once she'd finished, she went back to the living room and watched them finish a game of animal pairs. 'Time for bed after this game.'

Ryan gathered the final pair of animals and counted his score. He leaped on Jack's lap and put his arms around Jack's neck. 'I want Jack to put me to bed.'

'All right?' Jack asked, looking her way apologetically. She nodded, feeling isolated and suddenly alone.

She wandered to the bathroom door and watched Ryan paste his toothbrush as Jack supervised, and then wandered back to the kitchen, feeling peculiar with nothing to do at a time of day when she was normally busy.

Ryan's laughter echoed down the hall from his bedroom, followed by Jack's. They always laughed together. She tried to remember the last time Ryan had laughed with her like that. Ryan enjoyed Jack's company more than hers. Jack was football, games and picnics; she was baths, tidying and manners.

She put the coffee on and watched the dark liquid drip from the filter into the glass jug.

Jack roused her from her meditation when he entered the kitchen. 'Is Ryan ready for me to say goodnight?'

'He fell asleep while I read to him.'

'Oh.' She went to his room and stood beside the bed. Staring at her son's peaceful expression, she smoothed the hair off his forehead. She bent and kissed his soft, plump cheek, smelling the peppermint toothpaste on his breath. He was washed, changed and asleep — and it was all Jack's doing.

Later, Melanie lay in bed staring at the shadows on the ceiling. She kept turning over the problem of what she could do. She wanted to leave the town before the trouble really started, but she didn't want to take Ryan away from Jack. There was only one possibility — Jack would have to come with them.

She grabbed her mobile phone from the bedside table and selected his number. She chewed the inside of her cheek as she listened to the phone ring. 'Jack,' she whispered the moment he picked up, 'we need to talk.'

'It's the middle of the night. Can't it wait till tomorrow afternoon? I need to be up early for a meeting with that yacht company I've been courting. It could be a good contact if they recommend the hotel to their customers.'

'I've been considering my options,' she continued as if he hadn't said anything.

'Don't run away, Mel,' he said drowsily. 'We can ride this storm out together, you'll see.'

'Did you read those letters you took?'

He grunted with annoyance. 'People who write things like that are ignorant and small-minded. Just ignore them. We can ask Stephanie for advice about it if you're worried.'

'Like she's going to help us.' Melanie laughed grimly.

'You'll be surprised. She's a professional and if you go to her with a legal problem, she'll handle it.'

'Perhaps.' Melanie rubbed her eyes. Suddenly the day's frantic cleaning caught up with her and she could hardly stay awake. 'But now Ryan's older, he'll be a target at school. It's just not worth the risk.'

'Melanie, I want to marry you.'

She closed her eyes and imagined the handsome face of her beautiful golden-haired, blue-eyed god. But it was his little imperfections she loved most; the small scar on his chin from a football boot, his crooked bottom teeth. 'Come away with me, Jack. Let's start somewhere new. The three of us together.'

On the other end of the line his breath hitched. The suggestion had obviously taking him by surprise. For long moments silence hummed in her ear.

'What about Greyfriar House, my family?' He swallowed audibly. 'You're asking me to leave everything behind.'

She knew she was being unfair asking this of him but she couldn't bear to lose him. 'Ryan needs you . . . I need you. But I can't stay, Jack. I've lived through this nightmare before when people turn on me and I won't put Ryan through it.'

'Maybe you could go and stay with your grandmother for a few weeks until it all blows over? I could come with you. We could all go on a holiday together.' She heard a smile in his voice as he warmed to his subject. 'Where do you fancy going?'

'The problem won't just go away, Jack. My husband conned those people five years ago, and yet my name still made the front page on Friday.'

'I know what publicity's like, Mel. In my heyday, I was often in the papers and not always for my skill with the ball. People forget eventually.'

'Did you ever get hate mail?'

He released a frustrated breath. 'No.'

'Some things people never forgive — or forget.' The only way to make him understand was to show him. She opened the drawer in her bedside table and pulled out the grey journal she kept to hand lest she ever forget and repeat her mistakes. 'Meet me at your back door in two minutes.'

She put on her dressing gown and slippers and hurried through the balmy summer night across the yard and through the hedge into Jack's garden. The light above his door blinked on and he appeared silhouetted in the doorway.

He reached for her but she only allowed him a brief kiss before she pulled away and pressed her notebook into his hands before she lost her nerve. 'I kept a record of everything that happened five years ago.'

For a few seconds, Jack gazed down at the shiny grey book cover in horror as though she'd passed him something rotten. Then he squeezed her hand. 'I promise I'll read this, Mel. But before you make any decisions about leaving, go and see Stephanie and ask if there's anything she can do. For me?'

Melanie shrugged. 'Okay.'

It would be a waste of time, but she agreed to keep Jack happy. The appointment would have to be in the next few days because she didn't intend to stay much longer. If Jack wouldn't come with her, she had no choice but to leave him behind. Ryan would eventually forget him.

Maybe one day she would as well.

9

A few days later on Wednesday afternoon, Melanie caught the bus into the centre of town and made her way to Stephanie's office. Jack had persuaded her to come in to work at the hotel on Monday and Tuesday and it hadn't been as bad as she expected. Gossip about her identity spread like wildfire among the staff, but although everybody knew who she was, the people she worked with were civil, even if she did notice them giving her strange glances when she wasn't looking.

Melanie was cautious as she walked through the crowds of shoppers to the quieter business district where solicitors, accountants and estate agents had their offices. Nobody in town appeared to recognise her, probably because the photo of her the paper published was an old one in which her hair had been longer and tied back.

As she reached the metal railings in front of Stephanie's office, Jack hurried towards her from the opposite direction. He'd wanted to accompany her, but she thought he was busy.

'I caught you.' He smiled as he walked up, took her hand and kissed her cheek. 'I rescheduled so I could come with you.'

Melanie smiled back, but her insides twisted. He had such high hopes that Stephanie would come up with a miracle solution to set things right, but once the genie was out of the bottle, you couldn't put it back.

Once they were inside, Stephanie saw them almost immediately, unlike last time. When they were ushered into her office, she stood and actually smiled in greeting. 'Melanie, I saw the newspaper article. I'm so sorry.' She offered her hand and then indicated a chair. 'I'd no idea about your past. But I guess that was your intention.'

Melanie wasn't sure what she'd

expected Stephanie to say, but she hadn't expected sympathy and understanding.

Jack shook Stephanie's hand and she looked at them expectantly. 'No hard feelings. I've moved on.' She flashed an engagement ring on her finger. 'How can I help you?'

'You've seen the newspaper article . . .' Melanie suddenly found she didn't know what to say. However sympathetic Stephanie appeared, Melanie was uncomfortable talking about the way people treated her.'

'Is there something we can do to make sure they don't print anything more?' Jack asked.

Stephanie clasped her hands on the desk in front of her and thought for a few seconds. 'Not without making a big fuss that would likely get you more bad publicity than another article.' She leaned forward. 'Look, I know of other people in similar situations to yours and I researched the effects of crime on the criminal's family when I was taking my law degree. Everyone feels sorry for the victim's family, but the criminal's relatives tend to be forgotten or suffer by association.'

'What do you suggest?' Jack's eager tone irritated Melanie. He seemed to think this was something he could just fix. He obviously hadn't read her journal yet, or he'd understand.

'Beat them at their own game.' Stephanie sat up with an air of triumph. 'Melanie must tell her side of the story. Gain public sympathy and turn the tables on the critics. Do it well, and there could even be a lot of money to be made. You've seen the sort of story I mean. They often get a double page spread in the middle of a tabloid at the weekends.'

'No!' Melanie froze in horror at the thought of cameras flashing and people watching her. She and Ryan would never have privacy again.

'Mel . . . ' Jack faced her and took her hand. 'This sounds like a great idea. You could use your journal . . . '

'You kept notes?' Stephanie said. 'Well done you. That'll certainly make it much easier.'

Melanie looked at her hands and tried to control the trembling inside. The thought of everyone knowing every shameful detail of what happened to her made her flinch. She'd never be able to show her face outside again.

'You might even get some publicity for the hotel out of the process if you play it right,' Stephanie said to Jack.

The two of them discussed ideas for a while, but Melanie couldn't listen; a dark chill filled her heart and her head. Jack didn't understand how she felt at all, didn't understand what it had been like. She must get out of there.

'Mel, what do you think?' Jack asked.

'Let's talk about it later.' She stood and held herself tautly controlled to shake Stephanie's hand.

As she headed for the door, Jack said, 'We'll be in touch, Steph. Thanks for the advice and good luck with your new chap.'

Jack caught up with her. 'Why did you race out like that?'

'I'm not talking to any journalists, Jack. I'm trying to keep this quiet, not shout it from the rooftops.'

'But what Steph said makes a lot of sense. Tell your side of the story, Mel — please.'

Melanie started walking; she didn't know where, she just had to keep moving or she was going to explode. Jack followed her, skipping between other pedestrians to stay at her side.

'Can't you get it into your head that I don't like people to know?' she said between gritted teeth. 'Why do you think I kept moving on in the past?'

Jack halted but she kept walking. 'You have to stop blaming yourself,' he shouted after her. 'How can you expect people to believe you're innocent if you don't believe it yourself?'

She cringed at the curious stares of the people around her. How could she have ever thought he would understand?

Jack stood helplessly in the middle of the pavement, the crowd of office workers returning from lunch flowing around him.

Why? That one word kept running through his head.

Stephanie had made good suggestions on how to handle the interest of the media. Why wouldn't Melanie even consider taking the initiative and beating her critics at their own game? Once people read her side of the story and realised the truth, she'd be free of a past she carried around like the Sword of Damocles hanging over her head.

He knew she had a problem talking about what had happened to her because she felt guilty, but she wouldn't need to speak to a journalist. Whoever wrote her story could work from the notes in her journal.

As Melanie marched away and he started to lose sight of her in the crowd, he stirred himself and hurried after her. She obviously didn't want to talk to him, but he couldn't leave her alone when she was this distressed.

He followed at a distance as she kept up a brisk pace as if she were headed somewhere specific, then randomly changed direction. Eventually she stopped and watched some children in a playground for a few minutes and then climbed on a bus that he knew would take her home. With a sigh, he headed back towards the business district to pick up his car.

He sat inside his Mercedes staring blankly ahead, at a loss to know what to do next. He'd skipped lunch to arrive in time for the appointment because he thought she'd need moral support. Yet the way she'd stiffened when he kissed her gave him the impression she wished he hadn't bothered. Stephanie's suggestion had merit, because if Melanie got the public on her side, she would never have to worry about bad publicity again.

He slapped his hands on the steering wheel. Did he mean so little to her that she wouldn't even put up with the attention of the media for a short while so she could stay? He'd lived with paparazzi following him night and day for five years during his footballing days and coped with embarrassing articles about his personal life splashed across the newspapers. It was a nuisance, but it wasn't the end of the world.

After starting the engine, he drove slowly through the town back towards the hotel. Melanie's reaction had shaken him up. She didn't seem to want to resolve the problem. It was almost as if she wanted an excuse to run away and leave him behind. When he arrived at the hotel, he stared out across the neatly manicured lawns and colourful flowerbeds and shrubs that he'd ensured were carefully cultivated back to their original splendour. This elegant manor house had been his salvation eight years ago when his own body's weakness robbed him of his dream. He'd spent what little money he'd had the sense to save on restoring the decrepit Edwardian building to its former glory, converting the place to a high-class hotel, then building a reputation and business to be proud of.

Could he risk leaving it all behind to follow a woman who might not even want him? What if he sold up and within a few months she dropped him? He'd lose everything he'd worked so hard to achieve and have to start again.

He wanted to be with Melanie and Ryan; he loved them both. But until Melanie stopped punishing herself and let herself be happy, he couldn't see any way forward for them

* * *

'Why hasn't Jack come over?' Ryan said.

Melanie caught the abrupt retort that sprang to her lips as she remembered the meeting with Stephanie. She paused for a second to compose herself while the sizzling of sausages filled the silence in the small kitchen of her flat.

'Jack's eating dinner at his own home tonight, precious.' *And we might never share a meal with him again*, she added silently to herself. The thought trickled through her like ice water and nearly brought tears to her eyes.

Ryan pouted and stomped around in a small circle looking at his feet. 'I want him to play with me.' Melanie's heart ached. Ryan would miss Jack so much and there was nothing she could do other than try to ease the split by being understanding.

'Sit up now, darling, dinner's ready.' She arranged the sausages and baked beans to make a smiley face in the mashed potato on Ryan's plate then placed it in front of him.

He poked at the sausage mouth with his fork but didn't smile. 'Will Jack come over later to say goodnight to me?'

'I think he's too busy tonight, sweetheart, but we'll have fun together. You can choose a game to play before bed.'

In the past the suggestion would have made him happy, but now he gave a resigned sigh. 'All right, Mummy,' he said as though he were doing her a favour. He speared a sausage on his fork and bit off the end without cutting it up. Melanie didn't comment. She didn't have the heart to pick him up on table manners tonight.

Sitting facing Ryan across the table as they ate, the kitchen felt empty without Jack. She hadn't expected him to come to dinner after their argument that afternoon, and she didn't want to see him. Not when he obviously didn't understand her concerns, despite the fact he'd got her journal. Even so, she missed his conversation, the sound of his banter with Ryan while she prepared dinner, the quiet familiarity of his presence. Jack had become so much a part of their lives.

As she washed up, she stared out of the window at the darkening sky over the stable yard. The upper windows and roof of Jack's house were visible if she leaned forward. Light from his kitchen window gleamed through the hedge. He must be there having his meal, exactly as she'd told Ryan.

She stood with her hands wrinkling in the hot washing up water and pictured Jack in his kitchen sitting alone at the small pine table against the wall. What would he eat? Something easy, because he didn't like to cook. He might even have gone up to the hotel and collected a meal from the kitchens there.

'Jack.' She closed her eyes as she whispered his name and a hollow desolate pain gripped her chest.

'Mummy, I'm ready to clean my teeth,' Ryan shouted from the bathroom.

Melanie pulled herself back from the brink of tears. She must be strong for Ryan. He needed her. She bustled through, cleaned his teeth and tucked him in bed. She pulled the snakes and ladders box out and they played on the bedspread until his eyelids drooped.

Once she'd kissed him goodnight, she wandered into the kitchen and found herself staring at Jack's house again. She dragged her eyes away and her gaze fell on the engagement ring still sitting on the windowsill. She placed it in her palm and looked at it, cascades of emotion twisting inside her.

Should she put it back on? The path of her life focused down into one moment, one action — put on the ring and stay with Jack. Or not.

She had no choice. With exaggerated care, she placed Jack's ring on the corner of the dresser, ready to give it back to him in the morning. Next, she fetched the bags from the hall cupboard, returned to her son's bedroom and quietly emptied his chest of drawers and wardrobe into a suitcase. She repeated the process in her own bedroom, stoically collecting the few things Jack had left in her flat and putting them in a plastic carrier bag.

All her other belongings she'd collect when she found a new job and a place to live. It was nearly eleven p.m. when she hauled the suitcases into the hallway, ready for the taxi that she'd booked to take them to the station in the morning. As she turned the light off, a knock sounded on the door.

She hesitated for a moment, a flash of fear passing through her. Could one of the people who'd written the hate mail be at the door — who else would knock at this time of night?

She clicked on the porch light and peered through the peephole. Jack's face filled the view. A flash of hope went through her but she tamped it down. When she opened the door, he didn't move, just stood there with his hands at his sides staring at her. 'Can I come in?' he asked eventually.

She moved aside. He walked past and wandered into the dark kitchen without switching on the light. Melanie followed him, leaving the lights off; it seemed easier to face him in the darkness. 'What do you want?' Hope flared inside her that he'd changed his mind about coming with her.

He looked out of the window to his house as she had earlier. 'I saw your light,' he offered as if that explained everything.

'I saw yours, too.' Melanie bit her lip

when he turned to her.

He looked past her to the engagement ring glimmering on the dresser. Even in the dark, the diamond picked up any stray light and glowed as if lit from within.

With trembling fingers, she picked it up and held it out. 'You'd better have this back . . . perhaps you can get a refund . . . ' When he made no move to take the ring, she placed it on the corner of the table nearest him.

'I saw your bags.' She nodded. 'You're going, then.'

'I told you, Jack. I have to.'

He gave an irritated sigh and glanced around the kitchen as if there was something he needed to find. She braced herself for another argument, but all he did was rub his face and shake his head. 'So be it.'

As he walked past her, a little spurt of panic made her clutch his arm. He stopped and looked around, so close that if she stood on her toes, she could kiss him. The light from the hall glinted off his eyes, turning them sapphire blue, his pupils large and dark.

'Please stay,' she whispered. Foolish, irrational, but she wanted him with her on the last night.

He looked in the direction of the bedroom. 'Ryan?'

'Asleep.'

By the simple expedient of walking away, Jack pulled out of her grip. For a desperate moment, she thought he was heading for the front door, but then he turned down the hall that led to the bedrooms. Crazy relief rushed through her that was almost worse than pain. She followed Jack as he went into Ryan's room and stood beside the bed. He stared down at the little boy nestled beneath the football-club duvet. After a few minutes of silent contemplation, he bent and kissed Ryan's cheek.

The plastic carrier bag containing his few belongings lay on the chair in the hall and he pulled the bag open and stared inside wordlessly. Suddenly he seemed like a stranger; normally he smiled often, but he hadn't smiled once since he arrived.

He stared at her, his lips tight, jaw clenched. 'I should go.'

Her teeth sawed at her lip. She didn't know what to say but she couldn't let him go. Once he walked out, she might never see him again. She brushed past him and led the way into the sitting room. It was nearly midnight and she had to get up at six to finish packing; she needed her sleep, but instead she whispered, 'We should talk.'

Jack dropped into an armchair and hugged his bag of things. Melanie sat to his left, seeing his strong masculine profile silhouetted by the faint light from the hall.

'I'm sorry,' she whispered. Jack released a long harsh breath but said nothing. She watched him, tried to commit everything about him to memory so she would never forget him. Gradually her eyelids grew heavy.

Hours later, she woke with a stiff neck in the lounge chair, pale light filtering through the rosebud-sprigged curtains. Jack and his bag of belongings had gone. In a surreal daze, she wandered through to the kitchen. Early morning sunlight slanted in through the window but it didn't sparkle off the diamond ring and set rainbows across the wall like yesterday.

The ring had gone, too.

When the doorbell sounded just before nine, Melanie hurried along the hallway, pausing to check her face in the hall mirror. She pulled open the front door expecting the taxi driver, so the sight of Imelda Summers flanked by Emily rather took her aback.

'Sorry to barge in unannounced, dear but we need to speak to you.' Imelda looked immaculate in a green silk dress with matching shoes and the under-stated elegance of two strings of pale pink seed pearls around her neck, teamed with matching earrings and bracelet.

Melanie opened her mouth then closed it again; Imelda had the knack of rendering her speechless.

'Hi there,' Emily added, and gave an apologetic smile.

'I'm just on my way out.' Melanie wanted to get rid of them quickly. She didn't feel up to facing Imelda's inquisition.

Imelda peered around her at the suitcases in the hall. 'You're leaving.' Melanie didn't miss the hint of censure in her tone.

With a popping of gravel beneath tyres, the taxi drew up behind Emily's car in the gateway of the stable yard and the driver climbed out of his car, calling out, 'Taxi for Mrs Marshall.'

'She's not ready yet,' Imelda said before Melanie had a chance to answer. 'Why don't you go through that gate, walk up to the hotel and tell them Mrs Summers sent you. They'll do you a lovely cooked breakfast on the house and I'll pay you for the extra time.'

The man didn't need further encouragement. He hot-footed it through the gate before Melanie had a chance to disagree.

'I'll miss my train,' she complained.

Imelda shooed her back inside as though she was a naughty child and followed her into the kitchen. 'There'll be plenty more trains.' She sat down at the kitchen table and folded her hands in her lap. 'I'll have coffee, half and half with hot milk and one sugar,' she said as Emily followed quietly and took a seat.

Melanie looked at the coffee maker she'd cleaned so carefully an hour earlier and sighed in resignation. She put in a filter, spooned in coffee and switched the machine on. 'What about you, Emily?'

'White no sugar, thanks.'

Once Melanie had put a cup of milk in the microwave to heat, Imelda pulled out a chair and patted the seat. 'Emily tells me you're leaving for good.'

'I spoke to Jack on the phone last night,' Emily explained.

The last thing Melanie wanted to do was justify her decision, so she kept her answer simple. 'I have to.'

'I thought you were engaged to my son.'

'It didn't work out. I'm sorry.'

The coffee maker sputtered as the last drips of water filtered through. Melanie jumped up, relieved by the interruption and poured three cups. She kept hers black; undiluted caffeine might sharpen her wits enough to deal with Imelda.

Imelda sipped her coffee then stared into the cup. 'It was that wretched newspaper story wasn't it?' She shook her head. 'I'm sorry about that. Marco overheard Jack talking to me about you, otherwise I would never have told him. Goodness knows what goes on inside that stupid man's head.'

'Has the locals' reaction been terrible?' Emily asked with a sympathetic smile.

Melanie looked down at her hands. She hated discussing her problems. Even telling Jack had been hard. 'I've had some letters making threats.'

Imelda's head came up. 'What sort of threats? I hope you went to the police.

I'm sure there must be some sort of law against that.'

'I don't like to bother the police. I'm sure they've got more important crimes to solve.'

'What else has happened to drive you away like this?' Imelda demanded. 'Have people been nasty to you? What about the hotel staff? I'll have them sacked if they've harassed you.'

A flush of embarrassment coursed across Melanie's skin when she realised nothing had actually happened to her. The hotel staff had given her curious looks, but the only one who commented was the slightly dim but kind-hearted receptionist who always crashed the computer booking system, and even then all she'd asked was what it was like to be famous. Apart from that, nobody outside the hotel had even recognised her. Melanie swallowed as the silence lengthened.

Imelda reached out and squeezed Melanie's hand. 'Is what's happened so horrible you don't want to tell us, dear?'

To Melanie's self-disgust, she nearly nodded, but she couldn't lie to Jack's mother and cousin. 'Nothing else has happened yet,' she mumbled. 'But it's only been a week since the article was published.'

She risked a glance at Imelda and caught the look of incredulity on her face. 'Let me get this straight,' she said firmly. 'You're packing up, leaving a job you enjoy and breaking off your engagement to my son because a few small-minded people have sent you objectionable letters?'

Put that way, it did sound ridiculous, but Melanie knew how terrifying the situation could become. She forced her head up to look Imelda in the eye. 'I've lived through this before and it might escalate and get worse.'

Imelda's delicate nostrils flared. 'Let me rephrase, then — you're running away just in case something might happen.'

'No!' Melanie expelled a frustrated breath. Like Jack, Imelda just didn't understand. How could she, when she hadn't lived through what Melanie experienced five years ago? 'I need to protect Ryan. What will happen when he goes back to school? He could be bullied — even the teachers might pick on him. I've experienced first-hand how cruel people can be.'

'So you want to protect your son,' Imelda said more gently. 'That I understand.' Melanie nodded vigorously, thinking she'd finally got through to the other woman. 'Ryan is the most important thing in the world to you isn't he?' Imelda said.

Melanie nodded again. 'Whatever it takes to keep him safe.'

'And make him happy?' Melanie nodded and Imelda leaned back. 'That's exactly how I feel about Jack. He may be a man, but to me he's still my little boy and I'll do whatever's necessary to make him happy. What do you know about Jack's past?'

Melanie blinked at the sudden change of subject but gathered her thoughts gratefully. Anything was better than discussing her problems. 'Emily told me about his father leaving and the effect it had on him.'

'Then you know I was all he had, as you're all Ryan has. But what has Jack told you about himself?'

'He told me a little about his football career and the problem with his knees that forced him to retire.'

Imelda nodded and raised her eyebrows enquiringly. Melanie racked her brain for something else, but she didn't remember asking him about himself. She'd been so wrapped up in her own problems and fears that she hadn't taken the time to find out what really made Jack tick. She swallowed hard and bit her lip.

Imelda gave her a disappointed look. 'You know about Stephanie, of course. That was my fault. I wanted to see him happy, so I introduced them. I thought she'd be perfect for Jack, but I think he only asked her to marry him to please me and thank goodness he didn't see it through.'

She paused to take a sip of coffee and Melanie saw tears gleaming in her eyes. 'You don't know about Marianne, then?'

Melanie shook her head. She'd never heard the name before.

'I thought you might have looked Jack up on the Internet. It's all old news now, of course, but there's quite a lot about him from his days of football fame. I know there's information about Marianne because I've checked myself.'

Another wave of shame washed through Melanie. She knew he'd been well-known during his football career, but she hadn't even thought to do a search on the Internet or ask him questions. 'Who was Marianne?' she asked softly.

'His first love. They were due to marry just about the time he was declared unfit to play any longer. Marianne obviously didn't love Jack, but rather the idea of marrying a professional footballer. She left him standing at the altar.'

Melanie put her hand over her heart and imagined a young, eager Jack waiting for his bride and the embarrassment and hurt he must have felt when she didn't arrive; jilted him at the altar.

'The press had a field day with that one, I can tell you. I didn't think he'd ever get over it.' Imelda pressed her fingers to her mouth for a second before she could continue. 'Although he carried on with life and appeared to recover, he's never been in love again. That's why I arranged for him to meet Stephanie, but you're the first woman since Marianne he's been in love with.'

Imelda leaned forward and gripped Melanie's sleeve. 'I simply can't let you walk away and break his heart again. If you must get away for a while, come and stay with me. There's more than enough room in my home for you and Ryan, now that I've given Marco his marching orders.'

Melanie rubbed her temples. Ryan

chose that moment to wander into the room. He stopped in the doorway and angled his head coyly. 'Hello, Matt and Sam's mummy,' he said to Emily. He looked at Imelda from beneath his lashes.

'Come here, pet.' She beckoned Ryan who shyly shuffled closer. Imelda took his hands and smiled at him. 'You'd like to come and have a holiday at my house, wouldn't you, Ryan?'

He jumped with a slap of his shoes on the tiles. 'Can we, Mummy? Will I get to play with Matt and Sam?'

'All the time,' Imelda said. 'You can sleep over with them.'

Melanie watched Ryan jump around with excitement and shook her head. Imelda had outmanoeuvred her and her chest burned with a mix of emotions, some good, some bad, all of them painful.

Ryan bounced back to Imelda and rested his hands on her green silk-clad knee, seemingly unaffected by her intimidating presence. 'If you're Jack's

Mummy, does that mean you'll be my grandma?'

Heat rushed up Melanie's neck into her face. 'Ryan!'

Imelda took his face between her hands. 'Not just yet, my pet, but one day soon, I hope.'

Emily looked at Melanie and rolled her eyes. Melanie forced a smile. It was either that or bang her head on the table.

10

To give Melanie time to unpack and settle into Hazelwood House, Emily volunteered to take Ryan swimming with her two boys and Imelda had him bundled out of the house before Melanie had a chance to say yes or no.

While Melanie unpacked her clothes and put them away in the walnut wardrobe and chest of drawers, Imelda paced around the large pink and cream room she'd assigned to her, straightening four small paintings of the River Dart that were already straight, and brushing imaginary specks of dust from the back of two pink velvet chairs by the window.

'As soon as you're ready, there's something I want to show you,' she called to Melanie.

Melanie decided to unpack Ryan's clothes later as she couldn't concentrate with the older woman clucking around her like a mother hen.

Imelda led her along the wide corridor and downstairs into a library stocked with shelves of ancient leather-bound books. The sun gleamed off the waxy sheen on the bookshelves and desk while the pleasant smell of beeswax polish filled the air.

'Here we are.' Imelda stooped and retrieved three buff leather folders from a cupboard. 'Hold out your arms.' Melanie did as instructed and Imelda dumped the books on her like a heap of laundered sheets. 'Some reading material for you.' Imelda arched an eyebrow at Melanie that was not entirely friendly. 'Long overdue, in my opinion.'

'What are they?' Melanie struggled to put them on the desk without dropping the whole lot.

'Jack's history, courtesy of Fleet Street.'

'Huh?' Melanie opened the cover of the top folder and realised they were scrapbooks full of newspaper cuttings, all neatly trimmed and glued onto the pages.

'They're in date order.' Imelda pointed at the spines, indicating rectangles of card inscribed with years and months. She walked over to a set of French doors and threw them open. 'If you're careful with them, you can take the folders outside and sit in the garden. I'll have my housekeeper Connie bring you a sandwich for lunch.'

A little bemused, Melanie watched Imelda leave and shut the library door behind her. Everything had happened so fast today. She'd woken intending to leave for Brighton to take refuge with her grandma, then Imelda swept in like a whirlwind — and now here she was, in Hazelwood House.

She wandered into the garden and sat on the shady swing seat under an oak tree, looking over the lawn. Memories of the first time she'd been in this garden flitted back, when she'd sat here with Emily watching Jack play with the three boys. She'd deluded herself that since then she'd got to know the different facets of Jack's personality. She realised now that she'd not looked beneath the surface at all and knew nothing of who Jack was or what he wanted from life.

Once she'd eaten the sandwich the housekeeper brought out, Melanie chose the oldest book and leafed through the pages. She'd expected all the cuttings to be about Jack's football career, but they started when he was still at school. Small yellowing snippets told of minor achievements such as winning a creative writing contest and taking part in the Ten Tors endurance hike on Dartmoor. The books didn't just contain newspaper cuttings either; there were programmes from school speech days, many listing Jack's name among the prizewinners, and not just for sport; he'd won academic prizes as well.

She examined a photo taken when he must have been about ten. He stood on the steps outside an old building, smiling, wearing a stripy school blazer and holding up a silver cup in one hand and a shield in the other. He looked like an angel with his golden hair and blue eyes — he hadn't changed much and anyone knowing him then would easily recognise him now.

When she reached the time his football career began, the cuttings were few and small at first, but as the months went by, the pictures became bigger and the articles longer. He was either hailed as a hero or vilified — there seemed to be no half measures for sporting heroes.

As he became more famous, the sensational exposés started: tales of women, being accused of taking drugs, which he denied, his diet, his exercise regime, his clothes. At the height of his career, the poor man obviously couldn't get out of bed in the morning without someone criticising him.

Eventually she found a photo of him taking a swing at a member of the paparazzi. She didn't blame him, with the weight of evidence in her hands of how much he'd been pestered.

Before she started the third book, she took a sip of her icy soda and kneaded her tense shoulders. Poor Jack. How awful it must be to have the world watching your every move. She'd only had a small taste of this treatment, but he'd put up with it for years. The strange thing was that she couldn't equate the man they wrote about with the easy-going, happy Jack she knew. How could he have gone through all this stress and be so laid-back about everything?

In the third book, she discovered the first photos of Marianne. A tall leggy blonde, similar in appearance to Stephanie. If that was Jack's type, Melanie didn't fit the mould, but then, she'd always thought he was too good-looking for her.

Marianne obviously loved the camera and the camera definitely loved Marianne. There were numerous pictures of her, shopping, jogging, sunbathing, clubbing, on Jack's arm and aiming sultry looks towards the camera ... Jack with his arm around her waist, Jack hugging her, Jack kissing her ...

Melanie's throat constricted with tears as she read the numerous newspaper reports of his aborted wedding. The press's pursuit of the truth was merciless, whether they speculated on the guilt of the wife of a drunken doctor accused of defrauding his patients or a young man publicly humiliated by his fiancée.

In the accompanying photographs, the desolation on Jack's face as he pushed through the crowds to get out of the church tore at her heart. She wiped the tears from her cheeks as she read the final reports of Jack's injury and retirement from professional football. After that, there were still a few press cuttings about him. One magazine ran an article on him buying Greyfriar House to convert into a hotel. Then nothing for a few years until the hotel opened. The local paper reported on the opening and printed a photograph of the Jack she knew, standing in the doorway, smiling.

She put the book down to blow her nose and became aware of someone standing just behind the end of the swing seat. She leaned forward and to her mortification, Jack stood there, casually dressed in shorts, T-shirt and trainers. She closed the final folder with a snap and put it on the seat beside her, feeling as though she'd been caught prying.

He tilted his head towards the scrapbooks. 'Mother's airing my dirty laundry in public, I see.'

Flashes of unwanted sensation raced through Melanie at the sight of him, the sound of his voice. She couldn't think logically with Jack around. 'Did Imelda call you?'

'What do you think?' Jack came around the seat, placed the books on the ground and sat beside her.

Melanie sighed. 'I need time to think, Jack.'

'Then think.' He held his hands up. 'I'm not stopping you.'

'I can't think with you here.'

'Perhaps you should ask yourself why.'

'I know why.'

She loved him. Melanie closed her eyes and concentrated on breathing. Even when she couldn't see Jack, she was acutely aware of him.

'Tell me why.'

'It isn't going to help.'

'I love you, Mel, and you love me.' The subtle emphasis he placed on the word 'love' reminded her of the times he'd whispered the word in her ear.

'That's not what my leaving is about, and you know it.'

'It is.' His emphatic tone of voice forced her to look at him. Casually slouched in the opposite corner of the seat, tanned, muscular arms and legs relaxed, a smile curling the corners of his lips — his presence wiped all sense from her mind.

'You're afraid of me, Mel; afraid of how I make you feel.'

'Don't talk rubbish!' She stood up and glared at him in annoyance. 'I need to find a safe place for Ryan and me.'

'This *is* a safe place.'

Melanie glanced around the quiet, sunny garden in frustration, her thoughts running rings around her head. She couldn't think what to say.

'Look. I'm sorry I hurt you. That was never my intention, but I can't stay here — not now people know who I am.'

'Why?'

'Blast it, Jack — don't keep asking me why!'

Melanie stomped off towards the house and didn't look over her shoulder. What did the man mean — she was afraid of him? She'd never heard anything so stupid in her life.

* * *

Jack's heart raced from just being close to Melanie. Thank goodness she'd gone

261

inside the house because the urge to pull her into his arms had been almost unbearable. A few hours ago, he thought he'd lost her forever, and now here she was, in the home where he'd grown up.

He rubbed the sweat off his face with the back of his hand, rescued the remains of her soda from the small table beside the swing seat and downed it in one.

He hadn't intended to make Melanie cross, just to make her think. He needed to shake her up, break her out of her usual pattern of behaviour, make her mentally stand back and look at her situation objectively rather than being ruled by the fear she'd carried forward from the past.

As he placed the glass back on the table, his gaze fell to the three scrapbooks his mother insisted on hoarding. Why did women have to hang on to everything? He'd thrown out all reminders of his past long ago. He grabbed the books up and dumped them on the seat beside him, opened one at random and flicked through the pages. Sensationalist headlines he'd forgotten jumped out at him, making him shake his head. What a load of tripe they'd written about him. It was like reading about someone he didn't know.

Although the editorial was inaccurate, the photographs did make him pause. Every picture took him back to a time and place he'd almost forgotten. Snapshots of a different life. When he found a photograph of Marianne, a shadow of the pain and anger he had felt in the past rushed through him. Amazing how revisiting the past stirred up old emotions.

He closed the book and tossed it back on the seat. Maybe he could persuade his mother to have a ceremonial burning of the books as an example to Melanie. After his football career ended and he lost Marianne, a wise friend told him to draw a line beneath the past, find a new direction and move on. Nobody had helped Melanie do that yet. He hoped it wasn't too late for her to start again.

If he burned the scrapbooks, he would try to persuade her to burn her journal. He'd read her heartbreaking notes and hated to think of the distress she'd suffered, but talking about it and rehashing the past would only make her feel worse.

His only hope of keeping her was to help her move on.

*   *   *

While Jack and his mother sat in the shade of the oak tree chatting, Melanie unpacked Ryan's clothes. When Melanie found herself standing at the bedroom window staring at Jack lounging in his chair, all tanned and relaxed, she gave herself a mental shake and got back to work. She promised herself she wouldn't look out of the window again until she was finished.

Despite her good intentions, she didn't achieve her goal. Within a few minutes, the delighted squeals and shouts of three small boys drew her back to stare into the garden. Ryan, Sam and Matt all gathered around Jack, shouting and jumping about as Emily strolled across the garden to join them.

Melanie rubbed her temples. This was what she feared most. Last night, she'd gone through the difficult task of making the break with Jack and started to ease Ryan back into their old routine, and now she'd have to start again.

If you decide to leave, a little voice said inside her head.

Everything had seemed so clear-cut when the nasty letters arrived and she'd resolved to go. The hate mail was the first stage in a scenario she'd experienced before. The letters were usually followed up by verbal attacks — but as Imelda so succinctly pointed out earlier, nothing else had happened yet.

After exhausting the boys playing football in the heat of the afternoon, Jack was still around at dinnertime, looking fresh and cool after a shower and change of clothes.

'Don't you have a hotel to run?' she asked as he sat beside her at the dinner table and rested a negligent hand on the back of her chair.

He slanted her a grin, leaned closer and whispered, 'You're still afraid of me.'

Annoyance tensed her muscles and she told herself the heat spreading through her body was due to anger. She gave his hand on the back of her chair a pointed look and he raised his eyebrows but didn't move it until the food was served.

Why couldn't he sit at the opposite side of the table — anywhere but beside her, where she could smell the spicy fragrance of his soap?

Ryan was so exhausted by the day's activities that he started to nod sleepily over his desert.

'Excuse me, Imelda.' Melanie placed her napkin on the table and looked at her son. 'I think someone needs his bed.'

'He's had a busy day.' Imelda reached over and stroked back the hair from Ryan's forehead. 'Off to bed with you, sleepyhead. I'll see you tomorrow.'

Ryan gave Imelda a sleepy smile and there was genuine affection in the look. Melanie suppressed a sigh. Her options were narrowing by the minute. Taking Ryan from one person he loved was distressing; taking him away from a whole surrogate family would be impossible.

With a sinking feeling, Melanie realised this must have been Imelda's plan all along. The excuse that staying at Hazelwood House would give Melanie time to think was a ruse.

Melanie walked Ryan upstairs, prepared him for bed and tucked him in. Jack appeared at the bedroom door and rested a hand on either side of the doorframe.

'This was my room when I was a boy.' He wandered in and gently ruffled Ryan's hair. 'I'm glad you didn't take him away. I'd miss him more than you can imagine.'

She looked down at her sleeping son, suddenly ashamed. She'd thought about how much Ryan would miss Jack and how she could ease the parting for him. She hadn't given Jack's feelings for Ryan any consideration.

'I'm sorry,' she mumbled. 'I didn't think.'

'About me, you mean?' he said flatly.

She moved closer to him, drawn against her will. But he turned his back and ambled off around the room, touching the furniture, opening drawers, straightening a picture of the England football team that won the World Cup in 1966.

She moved up beside him to stare at the old black and white photo. 'I'm sorry, Jack. I never wanted to hurt you.'

'You didn't even consider my feelings, did you? You didn't even really consider Ryan's.'

At her son's name, her breath hitched. 'Of course I did. He's the most important thing — '

'You keep telling yourself that because

you can't face the fact that you're the one running away, and you don't even know what you're running from any more, do you?' He raised a hand towards her face, but curled his fingers into a fist and let it drop.

Melanie couldn't bear his cold distance. He was normally so caring, holding her, touching her in casual ways she hadn't even appreciated until he stopped. She reached for him and he stepped back, his eyes angry. 'No touching, Melanie — I can't do this any more. One minute you want me, the next you don't. Just tell me the truth. What are you really running away from?'

'You know — '

He raised a hand. 'The truth. Then we'll talk again.'

He turned and walked away without looking back. Melanie swayed slightly as she stared after him, the burning heat in her chest unable to melt her frozen heart. After a couple of minutes, the front door slammed and she heard the roar of his car engine, then the spitting of gravel as he drove away.

Leaving him had hurt, but him walking out on her was agony.

* * *

Jack didn't visit the following day.

Melanie paced around the house, looking for something to clean, but the housekeeper kept the place immaculate. When she went to help with lunch, the food was already prepared. She couldn't even spend her time with Ryan as he'd gone to Emily's house to play with Sam and Matt.

Imelda went out after lunch without asking Melanie if she wanted to accompany her. Having nothing to do was unusual and disturbing, and it left far too much time to think. She fetched her journal from the bedside-table drawer, where she always kept it wherever she stayed, and settled on the swing seat with the book in her lap. She looked at the shiny grey cover, unmarked, no title, nothing to give away the pain and anguish held between the covers.

When she was a child and did something wrong, her mother had made her write the offence in a book so she would remember her mistakes and not repeat them. Using that lesson, she'd kept a record of the troubles with Marcus so she would never forget those dark days.

Instead of reading her notes, she found her gaze drift off towards the distant purple peaks of Dartmoor where two buzzards glided in lazy circles against the blue sky. Imelda was right; nothing bad had happened to her since the poisonous letters arrived. She was planning to run away just in case things became uncomfortable. Viewed that way, her behaviour sounded cowardly and stupid.

And Jack was right, too — this was a safe place for her son and no one had been offensive or threatened them. She had no reason to leave and every reason to stay, because Jack was here and she wanted him so much she ached for him.

So why did she still have an inner compulsion to rush upstairs, pack her bag and run away?

11

Imelda arrived back shortly before dinner with shopping bags and a smile. 'How've you been, dear? I thought you looked a bit peaky earlier,' she said as she took her seat for dinner. Melanie wished she hadn't agreed that Ryan could stay over at Emily's. Being alone with Jack's mother and her perceptive looks made her uncomfortable.

'I'm fine. Is Jack coming over for dinner?' Melanie assumed he'd been busy in the hotel that day, especially as she was absent from her job.

'Oh, no. He was invited for a day on one of those enormous yachts. Janelle Constantis invited him personally.'

A flash of unwelcome jealousy made Melanie pause as she pulled out her chair. 'Who's Janelle whatshername?'

'Jack's been angling for this yacht manufacturer to recommend Greyfriar

House to their clients. Well, Janelle owns the company.' She winked at Melanie. 'My Jack's always been able to charm the ladies. He'll have that recommendation in the bag by the time he finishes wining and dining her tonight.'

'Oh.' Melanie stared at Imelda's smug smile as the woman flapped her napkin over her oyster linen skirt.

* * *

Much later, when the house was silent and Imelda had retired, Melanie stared out of her bedroom window over the front garden, sleep evading her. Although Ryan wasn't there and she'd missed helping him get ready for bed, all her thoughts were of Jack.

If he came over tomorrow and again asked why she wanted to leave, she still wouldn't have an answer for him. Frustrated tears filled her eyes. How could she tell him when she didn't know herself?

As she stared down the dark drive, headlights flashed through the rhododendrons. She clutched the windowsill, part of her hoping it was Jack, part terrified it would be and she couldn't answer his question.

The security light over the front door lit as his silver Mercedes swung around and parked. Melanie dropped the curtain back in place and watched through a small gap as he climbed out, locked the car and disappeared around the side of the house.

Melanie opened her bedroom door a crack and listened. The house was so big that from here, she couldn't hear noises downstairs. She walked along the hall to the head of the stairs and heard the clatter of cutlery.

Maybe she should be honest with Jack and admit she didn't know the true reason her gut instinct told her to leave. She hesitated, then descended, her bare feet silent on the thick carpet. He had his back to her as she walked through the kitchen door. She stopped with the table between them. 'Jack.'

He visibly started and coffee sloshed from the pot he held onto the counter. He glanced at her over his shoulder. 'What are you doing up?'

He still had his jacket on, but his tie hung loose around his neck, the top two buttons of his shirt unfastened.

'I can't sleep.'

'Guilty conscience?' he asked with a wry smile.

'You were right. Ryan and I are safe with your family . . . '

Jack brought his coffee to the table and indicated she should sit opposite him. He sipped and compressed his lips before speaking. 'I'm sorry about last night. I shouldn't have said you don't think about Ryan. That was unfair. I know you love him.'

'I try my best for him, but I've made so many mistakes.'

'You can only do your best.'

'Damned by faint praise.' Melanie met Jack's eyes as he watched her over the rim of his mug. 'I've spent the day thinking about my future. I didn't have much else to do with your mother shopping and Ryan at Emily's.'

She waited for Jack to mention where he'd been. The silence was deafening.

'Any conclusions?' he asked eventually.

'You're still interested?' At his frown she added, 'Imelda told me you've been wining and dining Janelle somebody-or-other who owns the yacht company.'

'Ah.' Jack gave a soft snort. 'Presumably Mother didn't think to mention that Janelle is sixty and brought her husband along.'

'Oh.' Melanie felt foolish. She had known Imelda was stirring and still fallen prey to her insecurities.

'You don't trust me?' he asked with weary disappointment.

'It's not that. I just thought you might be fed up with me after everything that's happened.'

'What, you mean the way you want me, then you don't, then you do again? But I'm not the one planning to leave,

Mel.' He raised his eyebrows.

'I do want you. It's just something inside me can't accept it.'

'I told you, you're afraid of me.' He shrugged briefly. 'Okay, maybe that's not quite the right way of putting it; you're afraid of your feelings for me, afraid of committing and settling down.'

She fisted her hands in frustration. 'Why should I be?'

'You tell me. You're the one who's been thinking all day.'

Melanie stood and paced to the window, staring at her own reflection in the dark mirror of the glass. 'I just don't know, Jack. It doesn't make any sense. I know I was avoiding men because I didn't want to trust anyone after Marcus, but I got over that or I'd never have got involved with you.'

'Maybe it goes deeper, then?'

She turned to face him and wrapped her arms around herself. 'Deeper how? Mum and Dad are still happily married. I haven't got issues with that.'

But even as she mentioned her parents, the familiar numbness crept through her.

As if he'd read her mind he said, 'I think it's more to do with the way your parents and friends let you down.' Melanie curled her bare toes on the floor and looked at her hands as he went on, 'You need to forgive and forget and move on. It's been five years, Mel. Just because the people you loved in the past let you down, it doesn't mean that I will.'

Tears swam in her eyes and she sawed her teeth over her lip. Jack shifted in his chair. For a moment, she thought he would get up and put his arms around her but he stayed seated.

'Why don't you make up with your parents?'

She looked across to him. 'How do you know I haven't?'

'Your grandmother rang the hotel when she couldn't reach you at your flat and I had a long chat with her. Every time you read those distressing notes you wrote in your journal you relive the experience and make yourself feel bad all over again.'

'I mustn't forget. It's a lesson.' She roughly rubbed the tears off her cheeks.

'A lesson in what?'

'Not to let it happen again.'

'Who mustn't let it happen again?'

'Me. I must learn from my mistakes.'

'Tell me why you think what your husband did was your mistake,' Jack said gently.

'Because I should have known. I lived with him and worked with him and if I'd known — ' She pressed her hand over her mouth to hold back a sob.

At last Jack stood and came forward slowly, ran his knuckles across her cheek and then folded her in his arms. She pressed her face against his shoulder and sobbed as he stroked her hair.

'It wasn't your fault, Melanie. Whatever people told you at the time, it was not your fault.' He kissed her hair and hugged her closer. 'The only thing in this life you have any control over is how you live your own life. You can never control anyone else, or guess what's going on inside someone else's head.'

He stroked the hair back from her face and made her look at him. 'You need to let this go and stop punishing yourself. You can't love me if you don't.' He kissed her nose and her lips. 'And I want you to love me, Mel, because I love you so much.'

*   *   *

After Jack tucked Melanie into her bed, he lay on the covers beside her, an arm around her, stroking her hair as she finally fell asleep. He loved her hair, so thick and glossy. Not touching her over the last couple of days had nearly killed him.

Part of him felt guilty for upsetting her so much, but making her work out for herself why she wanted to run from happiness was so important, he'd had no choice.

The next stage wouldn't be any easier. Now she understood that she was blaming herself for her husband's actions, she had to let go of the guilt and burn that infernal grey journal. Only then could she really leave the past behind.

Her soft, even breathing told him she'd fallen asleep. He'd intended to go to his own bed once she slept, but he kept on holding her. He traced her slender fingers where they lay on the bedspread and wished she would put his ring on again. But she must agree to burn the book first.

*   *   *

The following morning after breakfast, Melanie stood behind a screen of rosebushes staring across the rolling purple hills of Dartmoor. Although intellectually she understood she was blaming herself for not preventing Marcus's crimes, it didn't change how she felt inside.

Jack seemed to think she wasn't to blame and should forget what happened and move on, but she'd been raised to take responsibility for family. Her mother and father thought she was culpable and, however unfair that might be, their opinion mattered to her. But why should Marcus ruin her life? Melanie fisted her hands and huffed out a breath in frustration.

'You're not going to hit me, are you?' The smile in Jack's voice released some of her tension. He stood beside her and put his arm around her waist. 'I've rung Emily and asked if she'll keep Ryan for another day.' He threaded his fingers through hers. 'I think we should have a ceremonial burning. I'll burn the scrapbooks of press cuttings and you burn your journal. I don't think it does you any good to keep reading those notes.'

Panic flared inside her. 'I . . . I don't think I can.'

He tightened his grip on her waist, pulled her into his side. 'You need to start somewhere.'

She remembered Littlechurch, the day she'd left her home five years ago, people watching on the pavement as she bundled Ryan into the back of a taxi and escaped. She had never returned there, not even to visit her husband's grave.

'Maybe I should go back to the place where it happened. I'm not sure why, but I'd rather start there than with my book.'

'We'll go today, then.'

'Are you sure you can spare the time? Who's looking after the hotel while we're both away?' She'd wrecked his personal life; she didn't want to be guilty of wrecking his business as well.

'It's only one day, Mel.' He touched her face.

The journey passed without incident, although it took a long time to drive from Devon to Kent and by the time they arrived it was mid-afternoon. Jack's Mercedes glided into the main street lined with old cottages that must have stood unchanged for hundreds of years. The church, the village hall, the village green with its duck pond . . . so many memories assailed her — and many of them were happy, from her childhood and the early days of her marriage.

Melanie thought she'd feel nervous, but as the car stopped in the street in front of the pretty beamed cottage where she'd lived she felt nothing but sadness. She remembered the day she and Marcus moved in. The plans they'd had.

'How did it all go so wrong?'

Jack reached and took her hand. 'Things have a nasty habit of doing that. All we can do is keep trying again.'

An elderly couple she recognised walked past the car and looked in curiously, Melanie tensed, but they only nodded and walked on. She leaned her head back against the seat and looked Jack's way.

'What did you do when everything went wrong in your life?'

'At first I was miserable. I didn't get out of bed for about a week, drank too much, watched lots of mindless drivel on television. Then I got angry, but the trouble is, when your own body lets you down, guess who you get angry with?'

'Weren't you angry with Marianne for not showing up at the church? She could have spared you that.'

'I discovered that I didn't care about Marianne as much as I cared about losing my career — and that was the killer.' Jack stared out the windscreen for a moment. 'My old school football coach was the one who set me straight. I wish he were still alive. I'd take you to talk to him.'

'What did he tell you?'

'Lots of stuff, but in essence he said two things that struck home: it doesn't matter how badly you lost in the last game; when you go out on the pitch, the only game that matters is the one you're playing now.'

'What was the other thing?'

Jack stared into the distance and

grinned, the look full of affection. 'There were too many cuss words for me to repeat verbatim, but paraphrased it was, stop messing around and get back in the game.' He turned his grin on her, and the burst of love she felt was so strong it unnerved her.

In silence, they drove a short distance down the road and parked outside the church. Jack opened the door for her and took her arm as they entered the gate and took the path around the building to the churchyard.

Marcus's grave had a polished granite headstone inscribed with only his name and dates of birth and death. When the stonemason had asked her to provide an inscription, she couldn't think of anything nice she wanted to say about him. All her anger towards him had faded, but she hadn't realised until this moment. However bad things had been at the end, there had been happy times. Maybe she'd give an inscription some thought and have it added to the headstone.

Jack held her hand tightly as if he thought she needed an anchor. There was no vase on the grave, so she laid down the bunch of flowers she'd brought.

Strange that she had loved Marcus once and thought she'd spend the rest of her life with him. A different life. She looked at Jack and remembered his old coach's comment about forgetting the bad game from the past and playing well now. Jack was her game now.

'Do you want to visit your parents' pub or the surgery?'

'I'm not ready to see my parents but I'd like to write them a letter.' If she was going to put the past behind her, that meant forgiving her mum and dad as well.

They returned to the car and went half a mile down the road where Jack pulled up beside the village green. Melanie stared across the well-kept acre of grass and the smoothly mown cricket pitch to the old beamed White Hart Public House where she had grown up.

The swell of memories was so poignant she clamped down on the feeling.

Jack reached into the back of the car and grabbed a sheet of Greyfriar Hotel headed notepaper out of his briefcase. While Melanie composed her note, giving her parents a brief picture of what she and Ryan had been doing over the past five years and where she was with her life now, Jack silently studied the view out the window, giving her privacy.

She hesitated over the final paragraph, then finished by saying she would phone her mother in a few weeks when she was more certain of her future plans.

Twenty minutes later, they walked across the village green and she waited beneath an oak tree that was reputed to have seen the Norman invasion in 1066 while Jack posted her note through the pub letterbox.

After they returned to the car, Jack followed her instructions to the final stop she needed to make. He turned left off the main street, heading south. When they arrived at the surgery, Jack drove into the car park and cut the engine. The squat modern brick and glass building, finished just before Marcus joined the practice, looked ugly and out of place at the end of a row of pretty country cottages.

'That's it?' Jack asked.

'Hmm.' Melanie felt an unexpected twinge of nostalgia. She'd worked here for seven years and had friends here — or so she'd thought.

He quirked his eyebrows. 'Maybe I should go in and ask for a reference for you.'

She tried to smile at his quip and nearly managed.

'I don't think I want to know what they'd say.'

She'd worked hard here and done a good job, but they probably wouldn't remember anything about her except the last few weeks of turmoil and accusations.

Strange how, when she thought about

the place, she only remembered those few bad weeks. So much else had happened while she was here, but it had all been overshadowed.

An older woman with grey hair and glasses came out of the staff entrance and approached the car parked next to them. She clicked her key to unlock the doors and glanced in through the window at Melanie.

She stopped in her tracks, her mouth open. Melanie tensed.

'You know her?' Jack asked.

'I used to work with her.'

The woman approached her car and opened the door level with Melanie's window. Then she paused and turned, her expression uncertain.

Jack switched on the ignition and lowered the electric window while Melanie sat stiffly waiting for some cutting remark.

'Melanie Marshall? I almost didn't recognise you with your lovely hair cut shorter.' She crouched and looked in at Jack with a smile. 'Who's this?'

'Her fiancé,' Jack answered for her quickly.

'Oh, well, that's nice,' she said pleasantly. 'I'm glad to see you've moved on after all that unpleasantness.' She crouched to look through the window again and frowned. 'I'm sure I recognise you from somewhere, Mr . . . '

'Summers,' Jack filled in.

'Summers . . . you're not the football player, are you?'

Jack smiled and nodded.

'My goodness.' She put a hand to her heart. 'My son used to follow your team — had a poster of you up on his wall and everything. I expect we've still got it somewhere. It's a shame he's not here, he would have loved to meet you. Goodness! Just wait till I tell him I saw you, he'll be so jealous.' She paused and then added, 'What do you do now?'

'I own a hotel.'

'Well, that's nice.' She patted Melanie on the shoulder. 'You certainly fell on your feet. Good luck to you both.'

She climbed into her car still smiling

at Jack, backed out of her space and drove away, waving.

Melanie released a breath she hadn't realised she was holding. 'I didn't say a word.'

'You didn't need to. She said enough for both of you.' Jack laughed softly and brushed his knuckles across her cheek affectionately. 'I'll bet that's not how you imagined the conversation would go, was it?'

Melanie shook her head. If the people here had moved on and forgiven her, maybe it *was* time she forgave herself.

★   ★   ★

Melanie was nervous by the time Jack came home from the hotel the following day. She still felt uncertain about destroying the little grey journal that held so much of her past.

After she put Ryan to bed and Jack read him a story, Jack called her into his bedroom. He beckoned her across to the chest of drawers. Laid on top were the three scrapbooks containing his press cuttings. 'I'm ready to burn these and get rid of the last tie to my past.'

'Your mother doesn't mind?'

He winced. 'She's not happy, but she understands it's important to me.'

Melanie opened the first one. The school photos and speech day programmes had been removed.

'That's all I've let her keep,' he said defensively.

'If she hadn't taken them out, I would have.' Melanie closed the book. 'I've got a box containing all the important things Ryan's done. I wouldn't let anyone destroy those. Things like that are important to mums.'

'Why do women hoard?'

'Nesting instinct,' she said with a sideways glance.

Jack smiled and the slight tension between them dissolved.

'You ready to ceremonially burn those bad old memories?'

Melanie sighed. He was right, of

course. Keeping a book detailing the worst time of her life in her bedside drawer wasn't healthy, she could see that now.

'Okay. Where are we going to do it?'

Jack slotted his scrapbooks into a rucksack and slung it across his shoulder. 'Go and change into something warmer. You'll need a coat and strong shoes.'

Melanie glanced at the window. Dusk had darkened the sky to purple. 'We're not going hiking now, are we?'

'Got it in one. Go on.' He patted her bottom and his hand lingered until the pat became a caress, then he dragged in a breath and shoved his hand in his pocket. 'Don't be long.'

After she changed, Melanie pulled the journal from the drawer, ran her hand over the cover, and only hesitated a moment before she went to find Jack waiting in the hall. He took her book and slipped it into his bag beside his folders.

'Matches, check.' He held up a box

and dropped it into the bag to join the books. 'Celebration drink, check.' He pulled a bottle of champagne from behind his back and slipped it into the bag. 'Rug to sit on, check.' He pushed a tartan blanket into the bag and zipped it up.

'No champagne glasses?' she asked.

'They might break. We'll have to drink from the bottle. I used to do it all the time.'

'There speaks the professional sportsman used to indulging.' She gave him a mock look of reproof. 'I thought we were getting rid of everything from the past, surely that includes bad habits.'

'A celebratory drink's not a bad habit; it's a reward for success — and it tastes even better straight from the bottle.'

He took her arm and they slipped out of the front door to avoid passing Imelda and Connie in the kitchen.

Rucksack over one shoulder, Jack took her hand and led her down the garden and over a stile onto a narrow country road. A hundred yards on, they turned up a stony track that led directly onto Dartmoor.

Dusk closed in, the shadows blending into the darkness as the two of them hiked up a small incline and followed a path towards a heap of rocks in the distance, silhouetted against the deep purple sky by the brilliance of a nearly full moon.

'We won't go too far. The moor can be dangerous in the dark if you don't know your way.'

He glanced at her and she caught the flash of his teeth. 'This is my old stomping ground, so I know it well. But I'll only take you to Carp Tor.'

He pointed at the heap of rocks getting closer as they walked 'There's a nice sheltered spot beneath the Tor where Emily and I used to build a fire and cook sausages. Think of the worst barbecue food you've ever tasted and you'll have some idea of what they were like — black on the outside, raw on the inside. I'm surprised we didn't kill ourselves with food poisoning.'

Melanie smiled to herself and remembered Emily calling Jack a big kid the first time she visited Hazelwood House. She hoped he never lost that quality. 'You're enjoying this.'

'Of course I am. It's an adventure.'

She patted his shoulder. 'I hope your boy-scout senses don't fail you, because I can't see a thing now.'

Jack pulled a torch from his pocket and snapped the switch before directing the beam onto the path. ' 'Be prepared' — I haven't forgotten the boy-scout motto.'

The last section of the path narrowed to single width and Jack suggested Melanie walk in front with the torch as he followed. They climbed the steep incline to the Tor and when they reached the top, Melanie bent over, resting her hands on her thighs, to catch her breath.

Jack took the torch and shone it into a sheltered nook beneath the pile of boulders. He unfastened the rucksack, spread out the blanket and laid out the other things.

She gratefully collapsed in the shelter of the rocks, hot from the hike up the hill, but with chilly fingers and toes. As they approached the Tor, Jack had collected a handful of twigs. He tore a few pages from one of his scrapbooks and heaped the twigs on top. Then he lit the paper with a match.

Melanie hugged her knees and watched the small flare as he busied himself ripping out pages and feeding the fire.

'This doesn't bother you at all, does it?' she asked.

He grinned at her. 'Nope.'

'So you're not really making the sacrifice that I am.'

'If you'd had to talk my mother round, you wouldn't say that. She won't let me hear the end of this for months.'

'Jack, you shouldn't have made her give them up if she really wanted to keep them.'

The grin dropped from his face. 'It's

not healthy for her to dwell on the past, either. All this business with Marco is down to that. She still hasn't let my father go.'

Jack crumpled a handful of sheets and tossed the ball of paper on the fire. 'The old man was never worth all her heartache.' He picked up her grey book and put it in her lap. 'Come on. Your turn.'

Melanie turned the book over in her hands, opened it at random and angled it towards the firelight to read a few paragraphs. It was actually rather boring. 'It's not very well written, is it?'

'I'm not agreeing with that comment. That's one of those questions women ask where a man's damned if he agrees and damned if he doesn't.'

Melanie laughed, but her heart rate picked up as she took hold of the first page and ripped. She felt light headed as she balled up the sheet and tossed it on the fire. It caught with a little hiss and burned blue. 'Look at that. My paper burns with a blue flame.'

She ripped out more sheets and they flared with little blue flashes among Jack's gold and yellow flames. Silently, they both worked through their books, the fire burning fast and bright with the mixture of colours.

When they'd both finished, they threw on the covers. Melanie's grey book bubbled and singed with a sickly smell before the cardboard inside the grey plastic caught light.

While Melanie watched the last of the flames die away, Jack uncorked the champagne. 'Don't mention the drink to Mother. I forgot to bring a bottle over from the hotel so I whipped this from her cellar. I think it was probably an expensive one.'

After the pop of the cork, bubbles cascaded over Jack's hand. He took a swig from the bottle and handed it on. Melanie held it for a moment, remembering the blue flashes, the bubbling grey cover. That was the end of the past. No more worrying. People had forgiven her, and she had decided to forgive herself. And anyway, she'd never done anything wrong.

'To the future,' she said and sipped from the bottle. Bubbles fizzed up her nose and she sneezed.

Jack retrieved the bottle. 'To the future.' He upended the bottle and chugged some down.

'I can see there's a knack to this indulgence business,' she laughed, starting to feel light-headed.

'Oh, there is.' He made her open her mouth while he tipped in some champagne — most of it ran down her neck.

After a while, he leaned back against the rocks and stared at the burning embers. Melanie slid closer to him and cuddled against his side. 'So where are we now then, you and me?'

'That depends on whether you're still planning to run away from me,' he whispered.

She sniffed the delicious fragrance of his aftershave and closed her eyes. 'No.'

He put his arm around her and

stroked her hair. 'I want everything or nothing, Mel.'

She pulled away and tried to see his face, but the fire had died back. 'What does that mean?'

'I want you to marry me.'

'Or?'

'Or nothing. I'm not prepared to go back to square one.'

'And if I say yes?'

'You come back to Greyfriar House and move in with me.'

A shiver of disquiet ran through her. 'Before we're married?'

'This is the twenty-first century, darling,' he told her. 'Nobody actually cares.'

Melanie rested her head more carefully on his shoulder and stared out at the black velvet sky curving like a star-spangled bowl above their heads.

'What if I move back into my flat — just to start with?'

'That's fine, but when we get engaged you have to make a commitment — to me and to Ryan — and live with me.'

Melanie breathed consciously in and out, tasting the tang of smoke on the pure moorland air. 'You know I love you, Jack . . . '

'You were going to leave me.'

The echo of pain in those words pierced her heart. She remembered their last meeting before she was going to leave, how subdued and withdrawn he'd been.

'I'm sorry I hurt you, Jack. Really sorry.' She turned her face against his shoulder and he cupped the back of her head, pressing her close.

'All or nothing,' he whispered.

12

A week later, Melanie and Ryan moved back into the manager's flat at the hotel, in time for the start of Ryan's new school term.

As she walked past Jack's house after dropping Ryan at school the front door opened. 'Mel, I've been watching out for you.' He beckoned her over. 'I want to show you something.'

She hesitated for an instant, a flash of nerves running through her before she turned up the path. 'Shouldn't this wait? No doubt I've heaps of work to catch up on.'

He put a hand on her back and guided her into the living room. 'Ryan will be around later and I want to talk to you alone.'

She knew what was coming before he spoke.

'It's the moment of truth, Mel. Are

you ready to marry me?'

'You haven't given me long enough to get back in the swing of things,' she said, but recognised her old excuses.

'This isn't complicated.' He put his hands in his pockets, watching her. 'You either want to marry me or you don't. If you don't, it's over between us and I want to know now.'

'I love you,' she said, a hint of desperation in her voice.

'I know, but that's not what I'm asking you. I want to settle down and have kids. I want to wake up each morning without worrying if it's the day you'll pack your bags and leave.'

He wanted a family!

She'd given up hope of having a brother or sister for Ryan. Tears sprang into her eyes and she blinked them away.

'Give me a week or two to find my feet back at work.'

'I'm not asking you to marry me tomorrow. I'm asking you to get engaged and we'll set a date later.'

Melanie imagined Jack with their baby cradled in his arms and a powerful surge of love nearly swept away her legs. She went to him and pressed her face against his neck.

Tentatively, he folded his arms around her and asked, 'Is that a yes or a no?'

She looked up at him and smiled. 'Yes.'

His lips came down on hers and he hugged the breath out of her. 'Two weeks,' he gasped, breathless from the kiss. 'Then you move in here.'

A strange swirling started in Melanie's stomach; a head-spinning whirl of excitement and fear with a hefty dose of disbelief that it was possible to be happy again.

'Come upstairs. I want to show you something.'

He took her hand and led her to the first floor. Although she'd been in his house many times while Ryan played with Jack in the garden, she'd never been upstairs.

He pushed open a door into what was obviously his bedroom, revealing a pine bed and matching furniture, the walls and fabrics shades of autumn browns. 'Redecorate in here however you want.'

The sense of disbelief swelled, leaving her light-headed. This would soon be her room as well.

'This is a lovely room. I don't want to change a thing.'

'When we have our first baby, we'll move out of town to a bigger place with a decent-sized garden where we can have plenty of outdoor play equipment — even a small football pitch with fixed goals.' He laughed.

'You want the back garden to be a football pitch?'

'Not the whole thing.' Jack scrunched up his nose like a little boy who'd been put on the spot. 'You can have some plants and a washing line and things as well.'

Trembling inside with the poignancy of her feelings, she linked her fingers through his and he pulled her out of the room and pushed open another door.

The second bedroom was slightly smaller, but still a good size. 'This can be Ryan's.'

'This one definitely needs redecorating.' She laughed at the thought of Ryan's face if he had to sleep in a room with rose-pink walls and flowery curtains.

'Ryan and I can decorate it together. Bring him over and we'll let him choose the colours himself.'

He pulled her towards him and rested his forehead against hers. 'I love you, Mel. In two weeks' time Ryan can go and stay with Emily for the night, then I'll give you back your diamond and we'll celebrate properly.'

* * *

She'd said yes!

Jack stood at his front door and watched her flowing stride and bouncing chestnut hair as she walked up the drive to the hotel and disappeared through the entrance.

He stepped back inside and closed the door, then stood in the hallway, staring at nothing and remembering the look on her face when he gave her the ultimatum.

He hadn't been sure she'd accept his proposal and hated the fact that he still wasn't one hundred percent certain she'd go through with the move into his house.

Although he was pushing her, he felt that he had to, so she didn't slip back into her old habits. If he let her re-establish the old routine, he'd never persuade her to take the next step. She had to shake off her fears and fully accept a new life with him, or neither of them would be happy.

So now he had two weeks to arrange the next stage of his plan and organise an engagement party. Once she'd accepted the ring from him in front of their families, he couldn't believe she'd back out on him.

* * *

The two weeks passed in a flash. Melanie spent most of the time sorting out problems that had cropped up at the hotel while she was away and packing up for the move to Jack's.

So much for getting back into her routine.

Ryan chose his bedroom colours and spent evenings helping Jack decorate — or that was the theory. In practice, he seemed to be painting himself more than the walls.

She'd taken Friday off work to finalise packing in readiness to move over the weekend. A few favourite pieces of furniture she'd had in storage since she left Littlechurch were being delivered on Monday.

Everything in her life was coming good, and she'd never felt more excited — or more nervous.

Standing up after a long spell bent into a cupboard extracting boxed toys, she stretched and noted the thump of her heart. When she kept busy, she forgot her nerves but they always rushed back the moment she relaxed.

The insistent beep of the answer phone pierced her consciousness. It had rung earlier while she was cramped in the cupboard and been unable to get out in time. She checked her watch and started with surprise.

How could so much time have raced past? The phone message would have to wait. She'd be late collecting Ryan from school if she didn't hurry.

She changed shoes, grabbed a jacket and hurried out of the door to jog down the hill. As she rounded the final bend and saw the green school railings in the distance, there were still a few cars parked outside as parents collected children, so she wasn't too late after all.

Ryan had a new form teacher this year, a woman she hadn't met but knew by sight. The teacher was standing outside talking to another parent as Melanie approached.

When Melanie arrived, the man

walked away and she approached the teacher. 'Hello.' She held out a hand. 'I'm Ryan Marshall's mother.'

'Nice to meet you.' The woman shook hands, frowning. 'A man has already collected Ryan.'

'What?' She froze, hardly daring to breathe. 'Who?'

'His father, I assumed, as Ryan ran straight into his arms.'

Jack! Her legs felt shaky from the fright. She mumbled something and turned away.

Awful memories flashed through her mind of the night Marcus took Ryan from his cot against her wishes before he drove his car into a tree. She paused and clutched the fence for support.

How could Jack give her such a scare? He knew she always made a point of being at school on time to collect Ryan. If Jack had wanted to pick him up, why hadn't he mentioned it when he saw her that morning?

After the shock, she didn't feel up to walking back and the bus she hopped

313

on seemed to take forever to wind its way through the traffic.

Eventually she disembarked a short way from the hotel gate, her legs were still wobbly, but her desperate need to see her son carried her up the hotel drive.

The car park was packed with cars and she blinked at them, confused. There was no function booked that evening.

As Melanie entered the front doors, a waitress strode out of the dining room with a tray of empty wine glasses. The murmur of voices punctuated by the odd laugh spilled out of the room into the reception area before the door swung closed.

Melanie hurried forward. 'Where's Jack?' she asked, directing her question to all the staff in the reception area.

The waitress paused and looked at Melanie with a frown, then nodded over her shoulder. 'In there.'

'Is my son with him?'

'Of course.'

A surge of relief propelled her to the door and into the throng of people. She stood on tiptoe and scanned the crowd. Jack's golden head was visible on the far side of the room.

Melanie threaded her way between the people, her gaze fixed on Jack. Imelda's distinctive laugh broke over the background rumble of voices, making Melanie pause for a moment and look round. What was Imelda doing here?

When she got a clear view of Jack through the crowd, she was surprised to see Emily at his side. Then she noticed Sam and Matt as they ducked under arms and around legs, droning like cars on a racetrack.

Jack saw her, lifted a hand and called, 'Melanie.'

After a quick glare at Jack, she went straight to Ryan who stood at his side — wearing a smart grey suit and red tie.

She knelt, caught him up in a hug and closed her eyes. 'Baby,' she whispered as Ryan squirmed to get away.

Melanie stood and looked squarely at Jack. 'Don't ever do that to me again, Jack. I panicked when the teacher said a man had collected Ryan.' She gripped Ryan's hand tightly, despite his protests. 'Why did you dress Ryan up?'

Jack grinned. 'He's a guest of honour.'

Melanie put a hand to her thudding heart. 'What's going on?'

'You obviously didn't listen to the phone message I left.' Jack shook his head. 'That explains why you're not changed.'

'Congratulations — again,' Emily said, raising her glass. 'Second time lucky, I hope.'

A shudder of foreboding passed through Melanie as she glanced around at the people. Now she had stopped worrying about Ryan, she noticed many of the guests were watching her. Stephanie approached with a dark-haired man and a camera flashed in Melanie's face — too late, she raised a hand to shield her eyes.

'Don't you remember what's happening tonight?' Jack said.

'We're getting engaged . . . '

But Melanie had imagined an intimate dinner alone at Jack's house, not a packed room of onlookers ready for a party.

'Melanie, pet.' Her grandmother emerged from the crowd beside her and kissed her on the cheek. 'Congratulations, darling. I know you'll both be very happy together.'

'Melanie.'

At the sound of her mother's voice, she swung around and stood staring like a rabbit trapped in headlights.

'Jack invited us,' her mother added defensively when she saw Melanie's expression. She looked pale and much thinner than she had been. Melanie felt a twinge of remorse that she had cut them out of her life for so long. 'We were very pleased to get your letter and hear you've moved on, Melanie,' her mother said. 'It's about time.'

Behind her mother, Melanie's dad

hovered nervously, a tentative smile on his lips. Jack shook hands with her mother and father and accepted their congratulations.

Jack and her dad started talking about football, accompanied by some mutual backslapping and laughter. Another camera flashed and left a dark halo in Melanie's vision. Somewhere a glass shattered. Her ears started buzzing. Melanie's heart raced and sweat prickled her skin.

How could Jack organise an engagement party without telling her? Surely he knew she wouldn't like this type of a surprise.

'Mel.' Jack took her hand. 'Are you all right?'

Sweat trickled down her neck. She looked for Ryan, couldn't see him. Then the three boys wove through the crowd towards her. Her mother bent down and ruffled Ryan's hair, handing him a small wrapped present.

She wouldn't let them gang up with Jack against her and pretend the past hadn't happened.

Suddenly Melanie couldn't catch her breath, as if the air had been sucked out of the room. She pulled her hand away from Jack and caught the back of Ryan's jacket. 'We're going home.'

'No!' Ryan struggled and wriggled.

The people around them stepped back, leaving her in a small clearing ringed by curious faces.

She hauled Ryan into her arms, ignoring the jolts as he struggled. 'Mummy, let me down.'

The crowed parted as she raced towards the door. Behind her, Jack called her name, but she didn't pause or look round. She had to get out of there.

Ryan started crying as she headed along the path towards her flat. Fat tears rolled down his cheeks. 'Jack, Jack,' he sobbed as she carried him.

Somehow, she managed to make it up the steps to her front door but had to put Ryan down to dig the key from her pocket. As soon as she loosened her grip on him, he escaped and raced back the way they'd come. Melanie sagged against the door, too exhausted to go after him.

Fumbling the key in her trembling hands, she finally unlocked the door and made it to a kitchen chair, where she put her head in her hands.

First Jack collected Ryan from school without asking her, then he arranged a party without consulting her — and he had invited her parents! She'd wanted her reconciliation with her mum and dad to be in private. Her world was descending into chaos and she had no control over anything. Even Ryan wouldn't do what she wanted any more.

The telephone answer machine beeped and Melanie leaned across and pressed play.

'Hi, Mel, I guess you're not there. I'll pick Ryan up from school today because we've got a surprise for you. Put on your party frock,' he said jauntily with a smile in his voice. 'Tonight is the first day of the rest of our lives together, and I want it to be memorable. Love you, darling.'

Oh, it was memorable all right! Now everyone would think she was a complete nutcase after the way she stormed out.

★　★　★

Jack stood alone outside the front of Greyfriar House, rested a shoulder against the wall and hung his head. He'd done everything he could think of to help Melanie leave her past behind and move on — but she just wouldn't let it go.

Her poor parents had looked desolate when she ran out and he imagined his expression had been equally bleak.

The pounding of little feet heralded Ryan as he came running back around the corner of the hotel, tears pouring down his cheeks. Jack stooped and the boy ran into his arms, pressing a wet cheek against his neck.

'Hey, there, little fellow.' Jack stroked

his hair, keeping an eye on the corner of the hotel expecting Melanie to be right behind her son. 'Where's Mummy?'

Ryan shook his head angrily. 'Don't want Mum — want to stay with you!'

Alarm coursed through Jack. Melanie doted on Ryan; if he'd rejected her in favour of Jack, she'd be devastated.

'Your mummy loves you, Ryan.'

In response, Ryan hugged Jack's neck harder. 'She'll take me away, make me leave you.'

Jack pushed Ryan far enough away that he could see the child's tear-stained face. 'Has she just told you that, Ryan?'

He shook his head miserably.

Jack released a protracted breath.

Melanie's mother had told him that she thought she had suffered a panic attack. Apparently, she'd suffered from them in the past. A few months ago, Jack wouldn't have believed that possible of his coolly competent hotel manager.

He ached to go after her but if he

went to her now, he'd be giving in and letting her slip back into her old habit of running away. But he'd reached the point where he simply didn't know what to do.

* * *

Melanie went to the bathroom and splashed cold water on her face. She must go back and collect Ryan, but she couldn't walk into that room full of people when she'd just run out like a mad woman. It had been years since she'd panicked like that. The last time was the day her mother turned her back and refused to speak to her in the pub in front of half the village.

She stared at the pale face and flushed cheeks that stared back at her from the bathroom mirror. There was no hurry; Ryan would be safe with Jack, and she trusted him and his family to care for Ryan as if he were their own. But she must learn to trust Jack with her own heart as well or she would lose him, she knew that. The only chance she had to make it up with him was if she went back — and now, before the guests left.

Besides, she needed to speak to her parents as well, or they would leave thinking she hadn't forgiven them. The past felt like a different lifetime. Jack was right — she must let it go and live for now, she knew she must.

Quickly, she touched up her make-up and ran a brush through her hair. She stripped off her jeans and shirt, then dragged the contents of her packed bag onto the hall floor and found a dress.

Five minutes later, she locked her front door and headed back to the hotel, her heart racing so fast it made her dizzy. She paused, a hand to the rough granite blocks of the stable to ground herself, and breathed deeply.

When she felt calmer, she walked on across the stable yard, concentrating on the click of her heels on the path.

What did it matter if everyone in the room thought she was completely loopy? The only people whose opinions really mattered were Ryan and Jack.

She glanced up and there at the end of the wall stood Jack, the shoulder of his grey jacket leaning against the stone as if he had been there for a while. Her heart flipped again — he'd been waiting for her! 'Where's Ryan?' she said softly.

'Inside with Emily.' He nodded back over his shoulder, then nodded at her dress. 'You've changed.'

Melanie stopped five feet from him and nodded, not able to get out the words she wanted to say. Tears tightened her throat and she swallowed them back. 'Sorry.' She looked down at her dress and touched her earrings. 'I thought . . . I hoped . . . '

'That I'd give you another chance?' Jack pushed away from the wall and came towards her. He halted just out of reach and opened his arms.

Melanie walked into his embrace and pressed her face into the familiar crook of his neck. She could smell the sweet powdery fragrance of her son on Jack's collar. 'I panicked.'

'I noticed.' He stroked her hair and kissed her temple.

'Everything just piled up one on top of the other and for a little while I was confused.'

A smile spread across Jack's face. 'But you will marry me?'

'Yes,' she whispered.

He dipped a hand in his pocket and pulled out the ring. 'I was going to make a big performance of giving this back to you, but under the circumstances . . . ' He took her left hand and slipped it on her finger.

She looked down at the diamond sparkling in the sun and remembered how it had spread rainbows across the kitchen wall in the flat. 'There really is gold at the end of the rainbow.'

Jack put a finger beneath her chin and tilted her face up to him. 'At the end of our rainbow, there's love,' he whispered and kissed her.

We do hope that you have enjoyed reading this large print book.

Did you know that all of our titles are available for purchase?

We publish a wide range of high quality large print books including:
Romances, Mysteries, Classics
General Fiction
Non Fiction and Westerns

Special interest titles available in large print are:
The Little Oxford Dictionary
Music Book, Song Book
Hymn Book, Service Book

Also available from us courtesy of Oxford University Press:
Young Readers' Dictionary
(large print edition)
Young Readers' Thesaurus
(large print edition)

For further information or a free brochure, please contact us at:
Ulverscroft Large Print Books Ltd.,
The Green, Bradgate Road, Anstey,
Leicester, LE7 7FU, England.
Tel: (00 44) **0116 236 4325**
Fax: (00 44) **0116 234 0205**

PROMISES OF SPRING

Jean M. Long

Sophie, who's in between jobs and recovering from a broken relationship, offers to help out her Aunt Rose in Kent. Reluctantly, she finds herself being drawn into village affairs. Keir Ellison, a neighbour, is heavily involved in plans for a Craft Centre, but there is much opposition from the older residents who have different ideas for the old chapel. Sophie is attracted to Keir, but soon realises he's a man of mystery. Can she trust him?

LOVE IN PERIL

Phyllis Mallett

1792: Travelling on the long journey from London to Cornwall to meet her estranged father, Hester is plunged into peril when her coach is held up. She escapes and narrowly avoids falling victim to smugglers, due to the timely appearance of Hal Trevian. Hal takes her to her father, but, instead of finding security, other problems arise . . . although Hal is always there to support her. Will their interest in each other ever turn to love?